DORIAN

KeKe Chanel

NDJ Publishing

©2024 by KeKe Chanel

All rights reserved.

ISBN:97984342023986

KeKe Chanel

PUBLISHING

DORIAN

Chapter 1

"Happy High School Graduation Day," Kelly shouted, running up to Dorian with her arms spread wide open.

Dorian wrapped his arms around her tiny waist. He didn't want to let go but knew their families and friends would have questions he wasn't ready to answer. Although they spent every minute of their spare time together, they'd never crossed into relationship status. His friends teased him about being in the *friend zone* with the girl he wanted to spend the rest of his life

—

with, but he and Kelly didn't want to complicate their friendship. The kiss they shared on Prom night still lingered on Dorian's lips. He was hooked, craving more of the girl he'd been in love with since middle school. They never spoke of their kiss. Kelly changed the subject whenever he tried. He eventually stopped.

Dorian and Kelly had become classmates in middle school after her family moved to town. When she walked into his seventh-grade classroom, his heart went pitter-patter. He didn't know what was happening to him, but it felt good. Dorian had just turned twelve and she was ten, having skipped a grade in elementary school. Kelly was brilliant.

All the boys vied for Kelly's attention, but she didn't seem interested in any of them. When Dorian went over to sit with her during lunch one day so she wouldn't be alone, they became fast friends. Each day after that, they would eat lunch together and talk about everything. Her intelligence intrigued him the more they got to know each other.

Dorian stopped reminiscing when he heard the softness of Kelly's voice.

"I'm going to miss you, Dorian Carter. Please, keep in touch."

Kelly squeezed Dorian harder. She held him tighter as if she never wanted to let him go. At that moment, Dorian fell more in love with his best friend.

"Of course. Hey, I'll miss you too, but we'll always be there for each other. Just don't forget about me when you become this bigtime surgeon."

"Oh, stop it! I could never forget you, Dorian. You mean so much to me. How will I make it without you?"

"Hey. Don't talk like that. I'm not going anywhere. I'm here whenever you need me, and even when you don't."

Kelly pushed away from Dorian but didn't let go of him. She gazed into his deep brown eyes and saw her reflection in them. Her heart raced. The connection she felt with her best friend was magical. She couldn't imagine her life without him, but it scared her. Her parents' divorce probably played a huge part in her decision to keep things simple between Dorian and her.

"Promise?"

"I promise," Dorian whispered as he drew Kelly's body back to his. They'd held one another for what felt like forever when finally his mother cleared her throat to signal for them to go line up. Alice Carter was the high school counselor—loved by all of her students. Kelly Bishop was one of her favorites. She secretly hoped Kelly and Dorian would stop denying the energy between them and give love a chance. Alice saw the way they looked at each other. She knew what loved like when she observed her son with his best friend. Kelly was special. Alice hoped one day, they would give love a chance. Sadly, that never transpired.

"You two ready to do this?" Lucy asked, wrapping her arms around her two best friends' waists. The three of them were an unlikely trio but over time, everyone around town enjoyed seeing them together. It was clear that Dorian Carter was indeed a very lucky guy. Lucy—the eccentric one, Kelly—the stylist genius, and Dorian—the math whiz athlete. They worked. And for them graduation night was surely one to remember.

Weeks after graduation, Kelly moved to New York to live with her father for school and Dorian's heart broke. Why didn't he tell her how he felt about her? Would they ever see each other again? A million thoughts rushed his mind while dropping her off at the airport the day she left. They'd stayed up the night before talking and making promises to each other. Although Dorian wanted to kiss her again, he kept his hands and feelings to himself for fear that he would push her away by breaking her rule that they were best friends for life and nothing more.

They talked every day for a month until one day the number Dorian had for Kelly didn't work anymore. He was devastated.

Each time he called the new number he'd gotten from her mother, no one answered. Eventually, Dorian stopped calling. Weeks turned to months and those months turned to ten

long years. Kelly Bishop was the girl of his dreams, the woman he wanted to spend the rest of his life with—the girl who captured his heart when he was thirteen. She was also the girl who left him.

~~~

When Gemma Hendrix sashayed into his college roommate's condo dressed as Cat Woman for a Halloween party several years ago, Dorian was mesmerized by her curves until he got a chance to talk to her. Her intelligence and beauty reminded him of Kelly, but there was something special about Gemma. The kindness in her eyes sparkled when they spoke about the things, she was most passionate about, and Dorian admired that quality in a woman.

That night, Dorian and Gemma talked for hours. After their first date, the two became inseparable. Their love story was made for TV. Everyone envied what they had, yet Dorian still found himself longing for the girl he let get away.

What was it about Kelly Bishop that made him weak in the knees? Would their paths ever cross again?

One day, as he and Gemma held hands walking from a movie, he saw a familiar face—beautiful face—on a local billboard. *Kelly Bishop*, he thought. She had accomplished the one thing she went on and on about. Dr. Kelly Bishop sounded nice rolling off his tongue. She'd followed in her father's footsteps, was a scholar student at MIT, receiving several accolades and the pick of the liter from surgical programs all over the country. Dorian was proud.

"What's that smile about," Gemma asked. "Do you know her?"

"Oh, yeah, we grew up together. She was my best friend, but we lost touch a long time ago."

"She's pretty, and, from the looks of it,

very smart too. Black girl magic!"

Dorian watched Gemma do a little dance and fist pump, smiling the enter time. *Pure black girl magic indeed*, he thought.

"That's Kelly. She skipped a grade and that's how we met. It's good to see she's following her dreams. I'm proud of her."

Gemma noticed the faraway look on her boyfriend's face, wondering if there was more to the story of Dorian and Kelly. She knew how first-loves went, but her heart was already gone. Dorian Carter was a great catch and right now, he was standing next to her. Kelly Bishop was his past. She was his future. What they had was something she'd fight hard to protect and preserve. No one would get in the way!

Months later, when Dorian got down on one knee and asked her to marry him, Gemma knew she would do everything within her power to keep him happy. Still, something lingered in the back of her mind concerning Kelly. What if she and Dorian were meant for each other? Not that Gemma was insecure, far from it. She wondered if she was about to say yes to a man who already belonged to someone else.

Chapter 2

Dorian bobbed his head to the beat of the music as he drove carefully down the interstate. Glancing in his rearview mirror, he smiled, watching his son and daughter fuss over a game of car.

"I saw it first, DJ," Maysi shouted.

"Nah-uh! I saw it first."

"Cut it out you two. Stop fighting, daddy's driving. What do we do when we're in the car?"

DJ and Maysi looked at each other and then to their mother. "We stay as quiet as possible so that daddy isn't distracted."

"That's right, Maysi, sweetheart. DJ?"

"We keep still and try to be on our best behavior."

"Correct."

"But Mommy, Maysi is cheating."

"No, I'm not, Mommy. I cannot help that he's slow."

"Maysi Simone Carter, do not speak about your brother that way!"

Maysi dropped her head low. She hadn't meant to hurt DJ's feelings or upset her mother.

"I'm sorry, DJ. Do you forgive me?"

DJ didn't say a word. He stared his little cute face out the car window without a care in the world.

"DJ, I asked you an important question," Maysi said, leaning over closer to him.

Gemma and Dorian exchanged a smile. Their small family was perfect. Reaching over to grab his wife's hand, Dorian pulled it gently to his lips and kissed the back of it. He loved his wife, but deep down, something was missing. It didn't have anything to do with her not being a good mother, supportive, caring, loving, sexy, or having an intelligent nature; she was what most men dreamt of in a woman, especially a wife. *Maybe he'd moved too fast in proposing to Gemma before reaching out to Kelly.*

Sadness captured Dorian's heart. He didn't want to think about the reason for their sudden visit to his hometown, but it wouldn't go away. The death of his kid brother took them all by surprise.

Collin grew up a spoiled middle-class kid who didn't take no for an answer. His charm captivated all the girls. His swagger made him popular among the guys, and he was the apple of their parents' eye. Dorian also adored his kid brother—his only brother. A lone tear slid down the side of Dorian's face. He moved his hand from Gemma's and brushed it away, keeping his eyes in front of him.

Her heart ached for her husband. Losing a loved one was something Gemma had never experienced. She could only imagine and witness the grief Dorian and his family felt. She too had loved Collin very much. His death made Gemma realize that just because someone seems happy, it doesn't mean they are. Never would she have thought that Collin would be one to take his own life. He was young, rich, successful, and

handsome. It saddened, yet, puzzled her how someone could get so down on life that the end result was self-inflicted finality.

"Are you okay, babe?" she whispered. Gemma didn't want DJ and Maysi to concern their little brilliant minds with grown folks' business as they tried to do on any given day. Those two were wise beyond their years. Only seven and eight years old, Maysi and DJ could hold conversations with people more than double their ages. Gemma prided herself and her husband for teaching their children the importance of education and knowledge, but most importantly, communication.

Communication played a huge role in the Carter household. Each night, they all sat down to dinner and talked about their day. Gemma didn't grow up in a house where being heard was a priority. In fact, her family barely interacted at all. She vowed that her life would be different. Most people took the easy way out, blaming their childhoods for the lack, in their adulthood. Not her. Meeting Dorian was a breath of fresh air. They talked which she found attractive, although he was nice to look at. He listened when she used her voice. There was something sexy about a man who knew how to use his words—use his words to pour into others in a positive way. That was Dorian Carter, in a nutshell, the more time she spent with him.

Gemma fell in love hard. Now, she didn't know the right words to say to her grieving husband. She placed her left hand on the back of his neck, caressing it gently. She felt the tension there. *Being close to him will help*, she told herself. A touch could change everything when done in the right way.

Dorian wiped another tear and turned to his wife. "I'm okay, sweetie. Thanks for asking. I'll be fine once this is over with, and we can return home. I'm just glad you're by my side. I love you!"

"I know, love. And it's okay to let out your emotions. Don't try to be strong for our sake. We got you, babe. I got you. And I love you more!"

Dorian smiled.

"It's been a long time since we've been to your hometown. I wonder if anything's changed," Gemma responded to lighten the mood.

"Probably not. You know small towns don't like change. That's one of the main reasons I left and never had second thoughts about leaving. Sure, I miss my family, but that's it. I do also miss the beaches, though. They are spectacular."

Dorian knew his statement was a lie the moment he spoke it. He'd missed something other than the beaches—someone very dear to his heart. He missed her every day. Since the day he'd seen

her on that billboard, Dorian had kept a watchful eye on Kelly Bishop. He'd never admit that to his wife, but seeing his childhood friend
achieve the things they talked about growing up, made him smile. It also made him aspire to do the same. Secretly, Dorian owed his success to a silent partner—Kelly Bishop.

"I understand, babe, but your mom still lives there. You really should visit her more often or invite her out to stay with us. She would love California."

"I know. I'll speak to her this weekend. She'd older and I don't want the kids to miss out on forming a bond with their grandmother. Besides, what's keeping her there now?"

Dorian was still bitter about his father's passing only two years after he graduated high school. Because of the closeness he and his father had, Dorian couldn't bring himself to return home. It was too painful. No, it wasn't fair to his mother; he couldn't face his grief, so he buried it. Now with Collin's death, Dorian felt himself being sucked into a dark place. He had to pull himself out of it and quickly before it consumed him.

"Baby don't think about anything right now. Be there for your mother and I'll carry everything else until you're mentally prepared to take over. We are in this together, remember. Team Carter!"

"How did I get so lucky? You are one amazing woman. Team Carter," Dorian repeated, exhaling his angst.

Gemma blushed. "Why, thank you so kindly. I aim to please."

Dorian scanned his wife's body. "Yes, you do and very well I might add."

"Stop it before you start something we cannot finish."

"Oh, I plan to finish it and start it all over again."

"I plan to hold you to that, Mr. And I hope you can show me one of those amazing beaches you speak so highly of while we're there. Do you know I'm a beach connoisseur, right?"

"Is that right?" Dorian asked, knowing the love his wife had for beaches. Although they resided in California, the land of incredible beaches, he'd taken Gemma to a different beach every year since their wedding all around the world. But he'd never had the courage to bring her to his hometown.

"I think you know the answer to that question husband."

Dorian smiled devilishly, licking his lips as he admired his wife's beautiful sun-kissed legs.

Gemma sat back in her seat and rested her head. Hearing Dorian talk about his mother was bitter-sweet for her. Why couldn't she have a normal relationship with her own mother? Gemma had tried more than anyone would, considering the circumstances around the nature of the relationship she had with her mother. Still, she longed to gain her mother's approval. Janice Hendrix was a hard and cold woman who pushed everyone who tried to love her away. Gemma didn't know why, but she planned to find out one day. She wanted her children to know their other grandmother before they were too old to enjoy the love a grandmother gave so freely. Gemma was blessed she'd had her grandmother growing up. Without her, there was no telling what her life would be.

"Hey, you okay over there?"

Gemma regarded her husband. "Yes, I am. Just thinking."

"You want to talk about it?"

"No right now, but I do need your opinion on something important."

"Sure thing. Maybe when we get settled in at my mother's, we can go for a walk and talk."

"I would love that. You can take me to one of those beaches you miss so much."

"Deal!"

Dorian knew something was eating at his wife. He knew she wasn't as close to her family as she'd like. Hopefully, he could help change that. Hopefully, he could change a lot of things during his short trip home.

Chapter 3

Alice Carter stood from her rocking chair when she saw a strange vehicle turn down her driveway, heading toward her home. She put her hand up to her eyes as a shield to get a better look. The weather was beautiful, the sun shining brighter than she'd ever recalled it somehow. Alice took that as a sign that her Collin and Ford had found each other on the other side. Knowing they were together helped her cope with their deaths better. She missed them each so very much.

Lucy walked outside to join the woman she saw as a mother-figure when she heard a car coming up the road.

"Miss Alice, are you expecting company?"

"I don't think so, but you know the house is full of people these days. It could be anybody."

Alice sighed. She appreciated her friends, neighbors, and little family she had left for coming to check on her once word spread about Collin's death. Still, she missed her peace and quiet. That was one of the reasons she'd purchased her new home out in the middle of nowhere on the outskirts of town. After Ford's passing, Alice didn't have the energy to interact with people on a daily basis. She retired from the job she loved and closed herself off to the world. This was the only way to keep her mental health in check. She had the occasional lunch or dinner with friends and attended church on Sundays, but that was the extent of her being around people. Those who knew her understood and respected her wishes to be alone. Grief came in many forms—different for everyone. Alice's support system gave her space but was there when she needed them to be.

As the vehicle moved closer, Alice's mouth fell open with surprise. *Dorian!* Her baby boy had finally come home. Before the truck stopped, she was off the porch, down the steps, and grinning from ear-to-ear with her hands planted on her hips.

"Hi, Mom," Dorian said through his tears as he stepped out of the SUV he'd decided to rent. He'd missed her more than words could express. Seeing her confirmed that even more. When his mother embraced him, Dorian allowed his emotions to take over. He wept, releasing all the heartache and pain in his heart from losing his father and now his brother. It felt good to let those feelings out. It felt good being in his mother's arms. He wanted to stay in them forever.

Before long, Dorian's shoulders jumped up and down while his tears turned to sobs. He didn't care who saw. He gave in to his emotions, releasing the pent up hurt and anger trying to consume him.

Alice didn't know what to say in response to her son's actions. She did as any mother would do, consoled him as best as she could. She wouldn't let go until he was ready. She'd missed being able to wrap him in her arms. Alice didn't want to let go.

Lucy took in the sight with her hand on her chest. It had been a long time coming for this reunion. Dorian and Alice were once extremely close. She witnessed firsthand the effects his leaving had on her. Lucy did her best to make things easier for Alice, but a mother's love for her son was none like any other. Watching her struggle after Ford's death and how she watched Collin spiral out of control had been devastating. Thank God Dorian was back.

"Oh, baby! God has answered my prayers."

Alice wrapped her arms tighter around her son. She never wanted to let him go. He was all she had left.

"Ma, I can't breathe," Dorian managed to say.

"Oh, I'm sorry, sweetheart," Alice said with a chuckle. "Let me look at you," she responded, stepping back a few inches to admire her handsome son. Dorian was the spitting image of his father—tall, dark, and handsome. The dimples in his cheeks beckoned for her to squeeze them. Even with his full beard, they were noticeable. Alice caressed Dorian's face pulling it closer to her for a motherly kiss. She imbedded this moment into her senses for future reference, hoping it wouldn't result to that. Having her son home was something she'd prayed for. Alice hated to have her prayers answered under these circumstances.

"What are you doing here?"

The moment the question came out, Alice knew it sounded ludicrous. Dorian would never miss his brother's funeral. Their relationship was unmatched.

"Never mind that, baby. Why didn't you tell me you were coming? I could have picked you up from the airport. You didn't have to

spend money on renting a ride when I have two."

Before Dorian could answer his mother's questions the car doors slammed. Alice moved her attention away from Dorian to the people walking nervously toward them.

"Say it isn't so," Alice yelled in delight. "Are these two beautiful creatures my grandbabies all grown up?"

"Hello, Momma A," Gemma said, reaching up to hug her mother-in-law.

"Gemma, how is it possible for you to look younger and even more beautiful? My son is a blessed man."

"Thank you, Momma A. It's so good to see you again."

"Uh-huh," Alice cut her eyes at her daughter-in-law.

"No wonder I didn't receive your weekly phone call yesterday. Sneaky, sneaky!"

"Oh," Gemma said, turning her head to keep the older woman from seeing her amusement.

Maysi and DJ stood still glancing back and forth at each other. They knew they had a grandmother and saw her on pictures their father had around their house and speaking to her over the phone with their mother, but neither of them could remember ever meeting her in person. They were toddlers the last time Alice saw them.

Dorian kneeled down next to his kids.

"Maysi, DJ, this is your grandmother. You guys haven't seen her a long time, but that changes, today. Go give her a big hug and kiss."

Maysi went first, while DJ held on to his father. All of a sudden, the feisty 7-year-old little boy was shy. Gemma couldn't believe it. Dorian smiled, knowing by the day's end his son and daughter would have his mother wrapped around their fingers.

"Hello there Maysi," Alice whispered when the girl walked up to her. "I've missed you and your brother so much."

"Hi, Grammy! I missed you too," Maysi exclaimed, leaping into her grandmother's arms. "We have so much to catch up on."

"We sure do."

Alice fought back her tears. She didn't want to alarm her grandchildren with too much emotion.

"DJ," Maysi shouted. "Get over here and give Grammy a hug. You're being rude and Carters are not rude people."

"Well," Alice smirked.

DJ walked right up to his grandmother and extended his hand. "Hello, Grammy. I'm DJ, so nice to make your acquaintance."

Alice hid her excitement. Her grandchildren were perfect. DJ reminded her of Collin, especially his obvious charm.

"The pleasure is mine, DJ. Can Grammy please have a hug?"

"Of course."

Dorian's heart danced inside his chest. Watching the interaction between his children and mother was priceless—something he'd never forget. He interlocked his fingers with Gemma's. "Thank you," he murmured. It had been her idea for them all to come together instead of him coming alone. Dorian was happy to have them with him.

"No need to thank me, love. We are family and she should have a relationship with them. They need her. We all do."

His words got caught up in his throat listening to Gemma's. She was right. He'd been away too long.

"Come on inside. It's a little bit nippy out this morning," Alice said. "Don't worry, it'll warm up quite nicely in a few hours."

"You all go ahead. I'll get the bags out of the car. Mom, I love the new place. It's breathtaking," Dorian said admiring the rustic architect of the house and the fall colors of the big oak trees surrounding it. He could get used to the beauty of his mother's new property, but deep down, he missed his childhood home. Dorian wondered who'd bought it from his mother, making a note to ask her later.

Dorian saw Lucy on the porch and grinned. She was a sight for sore eyes indeed. He dropped the armful of luggage he carried and lifted her off her feet. It was good to see her. She'd been like a sister to him and Collin growing up. They didn't talk as much as he'd like, but he was grateful to her looking out for his mother in his absence.

"Luc, girl, you haven't aged a day. It's so good to see you!"

"Nice to see you too, Dorian."

"Thank you for taking care of Mom. I value you more than you know."

"No need to thank me. She's like a mother to me. I wouldn't know how to function without her here."

Dorian nodded in agreement.

"Need some help," Lucy asked.

"Most of these are Gemma's. You would think we were staying for weeks."

"It's a woman thing. You'll never understand," Lucy replied. "I'm so glad you came, D. Alice has missed you. She needs you. How long are you here for?"

"I know. Me too, Luc. Not sure yet, but this week for certain. Has she made any plans yet?"

"Good!"

Lucy sighed before speaking again. She was sleep deprived and tired. Listening to Alice's sobs each night after Collin's passing played on her psyche. Whenever she went home to get more clothes and personal items, Alice called to see what time she'd be back. Lucy didn't want to disappoint the woman she loved like a mother, but she was happy Dorian, and his family could finally give her a break.

"She's called the funeral home, but that's about it. Honestly, I think she was hoping you'd come to make them with her."

"Okay."

When Dorian and Lucy entered the house, the smell of freshly baked cookies assaulted their nostrils in a tantalizing way.

"I know she didn't," Dorian remarked.

"Yep, those are your favorite. I don't know how she knew, but she woke up early this morning to make them. I guess its fate."

"I guess so, and I certainly am not mad."

"Me either," Lucy admitted. "She hasn't made homemade chocolate chip cookies in forever. You know what they say, D?"

"What's that?"

"There's nothing like a mother's intuition."

"Is that right," Dorian said, moving quickly towards the smell of his childhood. His mother's chocolate chip cookies would put anyone's to shame and cure any ailment. She could make a hefty living selling them.

"Hey! No, you don't," Lucy hollered, catching up to him. It felt like old times—the good ol' days. She'd missed Dorian. Having him home would be good for Alice. Her too.

"Stop running in the house!" Alice shouted.

"Yes, Ma'am!" Lucy and Dorian hollered, halting their steps.

"Mom, you know those are my favorite."

"Yes, but my grandbabies get first dibs. Wait for your turn. I have to get their approval."

"Ah, man!" Dorian yelled.

Gemma loved seeing her husband this way—so childlike. She walked over and hugged Lucy. They didn't have a personal relationship, but anyone close to her husband was worth any effort on her part.

"Nice to see you, Lucy."

"Likewise."

Lucy felt terrible for not getting close to Gemma, but Kelly was her best friend. She saw it as a sign of betrayal, especially when she knew Dorian and Kelly belonged together. Those two were simply made for each other.

"Grammy, these are delicious cookies," DJ screamed, bouncing up and down with melted chocolate covering his face.

"They are amazing, Grammy," Maysi replied. "Can you teach me how to make them before I leave?"

"I sure will."

Alice's heart was full. She had her family back. She wouldn't let them go. They were all she had left. If she had to get on a plane to see them more often, she would without hesitation.

More cookies came out of the oven as the sound of smacking and laughter filled the Carter residence for the first time in a long time. Alice held back tears taking in the scene before her. She looked up to the ceiling, knowing God had answered her prayers. Now, all she had to do was get through the next few days, which would be hard. Alice wasn't looking forward to burying a child—her baby boy. No parent should ever have to experience this task.

Collin why? She pondered. Alice knew life

hadn't been kind to Collin as most assumed. He'd struggled a lot. She vowed to keep his secret and now, knew she should have gotten him some help a long time ago despite Ford's disapproval when mentioned to him that something was off with Collin. It was too late. Her baby son was gone, forever. And there was nothing she could do now to help him.

Chapter 4

Kelly looked up from her seat when she heard the flight attendant ask for their attention. She knew by the woman's face that something wasn't right. *Just her luck*, she thought.

"Ladies and Gentlemen, I'm sorry to inform you that we are expected to make an emergency landing at the next major airport."

Panic arose.

Damnit, Kelly mused. She didn't want to alarm or upset anyone sitting in ear's reach, so she kept quiet.

"What's happening," a male passenger questioned, leaping from his seat.

"Sir, calm down. Please remain in your seat. The pilot will make an announcement before we land."

"Bullshit!"

"Yeah, someone has to tell us something!"

"And someone will," the flight attendant said calmly.

Kelly leaned over and rested her head between her legs to keep from having another panic attack. They'd gotten more frequent lately, and she knew it was related to having such a stressful job. Being a full-time surgeon had its perks, but also lots and lots of headaches too. It was classified as one of the most highly stressful occupations to have. Sure, she loved her job—loved helping people—but she needed a vacation. Desperately!

The pilot's voice sounded over the intercom. "Ladies and Gentlemen, due to some serious mechanical issues on the right side of the plane, we have to take every precaution to ensure your safety. Please, remain in your seats and do as instructed by the attendants. We will land shortly at Hartsfield Jackson Atlanta International Airport. I'm sorry for any inconvenience but your safety, as well as the safety of my colleagues, is my first priority. Thank you."

Whispers filled the aircraft, but nothing crazy transpired. Kelly was able to calm down as she listened to the pilot's reassuring voice. Suddenly, it hit her. Hartsfield was an hour away from the town where she grew up. Her mother and best friend still lived there. They talked every day, and it would be nice to see them both since Kelly worked so much and hadn't taken a vacation in a while. *Maybe this weekend is a blessing in disguise.*

As soon as the plane landed, Kelly went to secure her luggage and called her mother after learning that due to a storm her flight to New York was canceled until further notice. *Surgery would have to wait.* Kelly smiled. Her mother would make everything better. Quickly calling the hospital to tell them her status and dilemma, to her surprise, they were very concerned and understanding about her safety.

~~~

Katherine Bishop was ecstatic as she pulled into the arrival lane at the busy airport. Her baby girl was coming for a visit. They hadn't seen each other in months, which felt like longer. Kelly—a highly successful, sought after—world-renowned surgeon, traveled all over saving lives. Saying how proud she was of her daughter was an underestimate. Katherine told anyone who would listen, about Kelly's many accomplishments. She and Alice talked constantly about their children, bragging of course. They both had secretly hoped that Dorian and Kelly would end up together. The day Katherine received a wedding invitation from Dorian and his fiancée Gemma was the day she gave up hope of him being her son-in-law. Still, she loved Dorian and wished the best for him and his family. Katherine knew that Kelly had strong feelings for Dorian. She knew the night her daughter came home from Sr. Prom with a weird grin on her face. But Kelly hadn't wanted to admit or express her feelings for Dorian because she confessed to Katherine that she didn't want to ruin what they had by entering into a relationship when she was going away for college. Kelly didn't want them to end up like them—her parents— unable to stand the sight of each other. Or worse, finding comfort in someone else during those hard times every couple experienced, especially being so far away from each other. Kelly didn't understand how people fell in love and ended up hating each other. She didn't want that for herself or Dorian. Being a surgeon was a copout for her. She didn't have time for anything serious. Yet, Kelly ached with loneliness. She ached for Dorian. It took her a while but once Kelly came to terms with her true feelings

43

for Dorian, too much time had passed. Knowing she'd given her heart to him when they were kids and now, they didn't have a relationship

of any kind. *I plan on changing that*, Kelly relished. From this moment on, she would contact Dorian and express the feelings she should have expressed a long time ago. Kelly hoped it wasn't too late. Her heart couldn't take it.

Looking around, Katherine scanned the baggage claim area for Kelly. Good thing she hadn't been too far away from the airport at a business meeting when she received the phone from her daughter.

"Mom! Oh my god, Mom!"

Kelly rushed over to her mother and wrapped her arms around her. They swayed from side-to-side, holding each other.

"Baby, you look amazing. New York certainly agrees with you. How long do I have with you this time?"

"As of five minutes ago, two days. Let's go. We have so much to catch up on before I have to leave. We will not waste a second."

Katherine did a little dance—her happy dance. "Well then, come on, baby! I'm double parked."

"Mom, you haven't changed a bit. You must want a ticket?"

"No worries. One of my former students is looking out for me."

"Is that right?"

"Yes. Now mind your business and try to keep up. You know this airport is a madhouse, today— madder than most."

Kelly laughed at her bossy mother and did as directed. Sure enough, Stevie Jones was standing next to her mother's car, wearing a huge smile.

"Hello, Stevie," Kelly spoke politely.

"Kelly Bishop. Girl, you haven't changed at all since high school. Good to see you."

"Thanks."

"Stevie, stop flirting and get on back to work. Thank you as always for looking out for me," Katherine remarked. The boy was nice looking but too shifty for her Kelly. He'd been that way since the first day she'd met him when he came over to their new home to introduce himself and welcome them to the neighborhood with his parents. He and Kelly walked to school together until Dorian came into the picture. Even then, Stevie made sure he wasn't left out. Katherine

admired the boy's spunk.

"Anything for you, Mrs. B."

Stevie helped load Kelly's bags into the trunk and waved them goodbye.

"Mom, what's Stevie up to these days besides working security at the airport? Is he married? Kids?"

"Why? Are you interested, sweetheart? I can make a call and set up a date."

"No, thank you. It's not that serious. Just asking is all. Plus, I know how to get my own dates. Besides, Stevie is nice to look at, but he isn't my type."

"Uh-huh," Katherine said, glancing at her daughter. "I know your type, sweet daughter of mine."

"What's that supposed to mean, Mom?"

Katherine didn't acknowledge Kelly's question with an answer.

"So, are you hungry? Want to grab something to eat?"

"Yes, I'm famished," Kelly responded.

"Where would you like to go?"

"Can we eat at Mack's?"

"That didn't take long."

"What?"

"It never fails."

"I cannot help it, Mom. You know how much I love that place. I blame you and Daddy."

Mack's was a great seafood joint in their town. The food was delicious, always fresh since it sat on the waters of Lake Lanier. The boats pulled right up to the dock out back and sold whatever the catch of the day was. Mack's was one of the places Kelly had to go when she came to town. It was where she spent most of her

childhood.

DORIAN

The town of Lake Lanier was known for its pristine beaches, amazing cuisine, and numerous attractions. It was a coveted tourist destination in spring and summertime. Kelly was happy to share with anyone that Lake Lanier was the place she called home. Secretly, she'd purchased a beachfront property there. One near and dear to her heart, which she planned to keep to herself.

"Mack's it is," Katherine said heading away from the crowded airport. Her phone rang and she connected it to her car's blue tooth.

"Hello, Alice. How are you today?"

The sound of Dorian's mother's voice put a smile on Kelly's face. She loved Alice Carter like her own mother.

"Hi, Kat. I'm well as to be expected. How are you?"

"I'm wonderful. Thanks for asking. What can I do for you, my friend?"

"Please tell me you're sitting down. I have news."

"I am, but I'm driving at the moment. What news? Spoil it!"

Alice's giggle was a delight. Kelly found herself doing the same. She covered her mouth to keep from making her presence known. Kelly wasn't particularly fond of the speakerphone. She felt it was an invasion of privacy.

"He's come home! My baby has finally come home, Kat!"

Kelly's eyes widened in surprise, yet she kept quiet. *Dorian's home*, she pondered. *And the same weekend as I am?*

"Alice, that's wonderful news indeed. I knew he would come. There's no way he would let you go through this time alone."

Kelly wondered what her mother was referring to. *Had something bad happened?*

A few seconds of silence loitered until Alice said, "I cannot go into any details right now, but I will call you later tonight once everyone settles in. We have lots to discuss."

"I look forward to it."

Katherine ended the call and turned up the radio. She knew Kelly wanted to know more, but didn't volunteer any information. Not until she spoke in-depth with Alice.

"Dorian's home," Kelly finally asked.

Katherine nearly ran off the road. *Kelly doesn't know yet.*

"Oh, honey, please forgive me. I forgot to tell you."

"Tell me what?" Kelly felt herself get a bit uneasy.

"Collin died a few days ago. Dorian's come home for the funeral."

"Mom! Why wouldn't you say anything before now? How's Alice? What happened? That's awful news to hear. Not Collin. You must take me to see her. I have to give her my condolences in person.

"Sweetheart, it slipped my mind. I'm sorry! Things have been quite hectic lately. We're all doing our part to look after Alice. God bless poor Lucy. She's been there day and night. Now that Dorian's home, we can let them catch up and grieve as a family—together. Lucy can go home and rest. I don't think it's a good idea to go for a visit right now."

Kelly immediately wanted to reach out to Dorian and his family during their time of bereavement but knew it wasn't a wise decision considering they hadn't spoken to or seen each other in years. Still, in her eyes, Collin was family. Seeing Dorian while she was home would be a welcomed distraction, but Kelly wondered what she would say or how he would react to seeing her. Things hadn't turned out between them as she'd hoped.

"Mom, I don't think Mrs. Carter or Dorian would mind any company from the two of us. In fact, I bet they'll be happy to see us."

"I'm sure you're right, sweetheart. But you do know he's married," Katherine quizzed. Shock and sadness swept over Kelly like a wrecking ball, although she wasn't surprised. Dorian was a great catch. Yet, hearing those words broke her heart. If only she had told him how she truly felt about him when they were younger. Things would be different for them all.

"Honey don't do that. Kelly, have your whole life ahead of you. Don't dwell on the past. You'll be gone in a few days—back to your life. Until then, steer clear of Dorian Carter. We will attend Collin's funeral and that's it. No hanging out with the family afterward. You're young, successful, and beautiful inside and out. You will make someone a great wife one day. Trust me."

Kelly wanted to disagree with her mother's demands but knew her mother was right. She also wanted to tell her mother the same thing about her getting back out there dating. It had been too long since the divorce. It was time. Her mother deserved happiness too.

Seeing Dorian with another woman—his wife—

wouldn't be a pleasant experience, Kelly concluded. Her mother's words made more sense. Running into or seeing Dorian Carter next to anyone who wasn't her, wasn't something Kelly looked forward to. *Damn, why do I have to be here now?*

"Mom, can I ask you a question?"

"Sure. You know you can ask me anything, sweetheart."

"How long have you known about Dorian being married?"

Katherine sighed. She didn't want to argue with her only child. They didn't get to spend as much time together as she'd hoped, but if Kelly wanted to know the truth to keep from making a fool out of herself, so be it.

"His mother sent me an invitation to his wedding. I've known for years, Kelly. My question to you, my dear, is how didn't you know?"

Words tried to form, but none came. Kelly knew what her mother was getting at. She didn't want to talk about it.

"Forget I asked, Mom. You should have said something."

"Why should I have said something? Isn't Dorian one of your best friends? Why was it up to me to tell you about his *big* day? You guys are grown, Kelly. Grow up and move on. I know you love Dorian, but he's married. Besides, you never told him how you felt. Men don't read minds and neither do women. I learned that the hard way with your father. Listen to me, and listen well. Stay away from Dorian Carter and his family. We do not want any trouble, Kelly. We both know that is inevitable where the two of you are concerned."

"Mama, stop it! Don't you think I know all that? I should have told him. I should have kept in touch.

I should have done a lot of things I didn't do. Please, can you be on my side for once?"

Kelly rubbed her temples to silence the headache threatening to knock her off her feet. Whenever she and her mother where around one another too long, there was guaranteed to be a fight involving Dorian Carter. This had become their norm since Kelly invited him over after school when they were in middle school. Katherine wasn't fond of Dorian in the beginning but learned how great of a guy he was once he became a frequent dinner guest in their home. Katherine knew Kelly was to blame for and Dorian's friendship-only relationship. Partly, she blamed herself for the chaos her daughter witnessed when she and her ex-husband went through their ugly divorce. Katherine also knew that the divorce had played a huge part in her daughter's singleness.

"We're here. Let's table this conversation for later when we are alone."

"Sure. Mack's is the exact same. I pray the food is too."

"Come on," Katherine responded as she got out of the car. "It is and you won't be disappointed."

Kelly caught up to her mother, interlocking their arms. Katherine placed her hand over her daughter's and leaned her head on her shoulder. "I'm glad you're home, baby."

"Me too, Mom. I've missed you so much."

"Stop it before you make me mess up my makeup."

"We cannot have that," Kelly teased. Her mother loved makeup even though she didn't need it. Growing up, they would play dress-up and her mother would do her makeup for any occasion. Katherine Bishop quickly became the town's go-to MUA, securing a nice nest egg that funded opening her own makeup studio. *Beat* was a striving and successful business. Now, Katherine worked part-time. She hired people she trained and trusted to run the day-to-day operations, which afforded her lots of free time.

Kelly saw many of her classmates and their families eating at Mack's. Being from a small community, everyone knew everyone whether they still lived there or not. Many people came up to their secluded table in the back to congratulate Kelly on her success as a surgeon. When Lucy walked in, squeals could be heard throughout the restaurant. The two friends ran to each other, hugging and rocking from side-to-side. People smiled, knowing that Kelly and Lucy were inseparable during their childhood years. Most of the people watching their interaction basked in the beauty of their friendship. Katherine Bishop was one of them.

When Lucy finally turned Kelly loose, she whispered, "We need to talk. He's here."

"I know. Mama received a call from Alice on our way from the airport. I've never heard a woman so excited before in my life."

"She loves him so much it's cute," Lucy said.

"Where is he?"

Kelly searched the room as if she were looking for someone.

"He's not here. Relax. Dang, you still got it bad, boo."

"Shut up," Kelly said, swiping Lucy on the arm.

"Hey! Ouch, that hurt."

"Don't try it! I barely touched you."

"Mrs. K, Kelly hit me," Lucy tattle tailed.

KeKe Chanel

Katherine's heart was full. She loved seeing her daughter happy and one thing about Lucy Jacobs, she made sure Kelly remained young and carefree. They took girls' trips every six months, talked daily, and kept it real with each other. They reminded her of her friendship with Alice.

"Hey, Mom, you alright," Kelly asked watching the tears form in her mother's eyes.

"Oh baby, I'm great. I just love watching you and Lucy. You girls have something most people search for their whole life. Cherish it forever."

"We do," Lucy and Kelly said in unison.

Lucy joined them for lunch, and they laughed and talked for hours. By the time they realized it, it was almost closing time for Mack's to prepare for dinner. Katherine spotted a friend she needed to speak with and excused herself.

"Girl, spill it! How does he look?"

Lucy couldn't contain her laughter. "Wouldn't you like to know? My lips are sealed."

"You're my best friend. How could you do this to me? And why didn't you mention anything about Dorian being married? We talk every day."

"It wasn't my place to tell you, Kelly. Dorian promised me he would before he ever got hitched. In fact, he went to New York to see you in person, so I don't know what happened because you didn't say anything about him coming and neither has, he. Next thing I know, I'm getting a fancy wedding invitation out of the mail and buying a fancy dress to attend. I thought for sure you of all people would be there. When you didn't show up, I figured you couldn't. You know—seeing as how madly in love you are with him and all."

"Don't," Kelly murmured, gritting her teeth in frustration. Dorian hadn't come to see her or called.

Something wasn't right. She had to talk to him to find out his side of the story. Why else would he say those things to Lucy?

"Before you get any bright ideas, she's with him. Their kids are too."

"Kids? How many?"

"Two. A boy and a girl. They are precious. You would love them. Listen, I have to run. Great seeing you, Kell. Call me later. I'll be up kinda late finishing up the obituary for Collin. Maybe we can have dinner at my house tonight."

"Okay. Do you need any help? I can come over once mom settles in for the night. We can hang a bit in private. Plus, she and Alice will probably be on the phone most of the night anyway. You know how those two are when they get on the telephone."

"Boy, do I ever. Sounds good just let me know, okay."

"Sure. I'll call you later."

"Cool," Lucy said grabbing her jacket and backpack. She hugged Katherine on her way out the door. The smile on Katherine's face was priceless, Kelly noticed. *Who is that man making my mother gush all over herself?* She wondered. *I'm not mad. She deserves to be happy.*

Kelly waited patiently for her mother to finish her conversation, but she was tired and wanted to go shower and take a nap before meeting up with Lucy. Glancing out the window, she froze. There he was, walking hand in hand, with a striking woman. *Dorian,* Kelly mouthed. As if he'd heard her somehow, he turned and looked in her direction. His eyes bow into her soul, yet she couldn't bring herself to turn away from the intenseness of his stare.

~~~

Dorian couldn't believe his eyes. *Kelly.* There she was right in front of him at their once favorite spot in town. *What is she doing here? Had she come to pay her respects to his brother?* A million questions clouded his mind. Dorian wanted to go to her—the girl who stole his heart when he was thirteen—the girl he'd give anything to make all his—the girl he could no longer have.

"Babe, everything okay?"

Gemma's voice broke the gaze between him and Kelly. Dorian didn't want his wife to see his former best friend, so he pulled her along the trail by the lake for the rest of their walk. His mind couldn't shake the image of Kelly. She was more beautiful than he remembered. How was it that she seemed to be aging backwards?

"Come on. We should get back before our children take advantage of my mother."

"Right," Gemma said with a puzzled look. *What did I just miss?* She turned to look behind them but what she saw nearly stopped her heart. *It can't be.* The person staring back at her gave a wave and dirty smirk. Gemma wanted to flee but didn't want to alarm Dorian or explain why. Her past had caught up to her—the past that could ruin everything she loved. Closing her eyes, Gemma hoped her mind was messing with her when she reopened them.

Whew, she thought when no one was there. Searching the area, Gemma didn't know what to think or feel. One of the things she'd heard about Lake Lanier was how supernatural it was. Many people lived at the bottom of the lake according to her research and listening to Dorian's stories. *Had her mind begin to play tricks on her?*

"Babe, come on."

"I'm coming!"

Gemma ran to catch up with her husband. She

jumped onto his back in a playful manner. Dorian carried her as if she weighed nothing, gripping her curvy backside along the way back to his mother's house. But his mind was still on the woman he'd just seen. He had to see her before she left. They had unfinished business to attend to, and this time, he wasn't letting her off the hook as easily as he'd done years ago when he went to New York to see her.

Chapter 5

Lucy and Kelly were in the middle of a heated dance party when they heard the sound of the doorbell.

"Are you expecting company this late?" Kelly inquired. "Wait a minute. Lucy Jacobs, are you holding out on your best friend? Are you seeing someone? Is it serious? I need answers, young lady."

"Slow your roll. No, I'm not expecting anyone but yes, I am dating. I was going to tell you about that later. Calm down!"

Kelly covered her mouth. She was happy for her best friend, wanting to know who this mystery person was. The doorbell sounded again followed by a series of impatient knocks.

"Answer it. I should probably go anyway. It's late. I know mom won't fall asleep until she knows I'm home safely. You know how that woman is."

"That I do. She knows you're safe with me, Kell. Call and tell her you're spending the night. We haven't had a proper sleepover in years. Vacations don't count. Besides, we aren't done with our talk."

"Yeah, yeah! I'll call mom while you answer the door."

"Deal."

Lucy couldn't believe her eyes when she saw Dorian standing on her front porch as she peeked out of the window. She backed away from the door and looked at Kelly who'd just hung up the phone with her mother.

Kelly threw her hands up. "What? Who is it?" She lowered her tone in case Lucy didn't want the person on the other side of the door to know she was home.

"Lucy, I know you're home. I can hear you. Please, open the door. We need to talk."

"Oh my god! What is he doing here?" Kelly felt her blood pressure rising. She looked at her best friend with questioning eyes.

"Did you set this up? Did you tell him I would be here, Luc? Is he the reason you wanted me to stay the night?"

"No! What kind of friend do you think I am? I would never do that. I don't know why he's here, but he is. What do you want me to do?"

The room started spinning. Kelly couldn't breathe. She sat down in a nearby chair, resting her head between her knees. Taking small, deep breaths, she began to feel better. By this time, Dorian stood watching her with a concerned look on his face. Lucy kneeled down in front of her.

"Kell, you, okay? Let me get you a glass of water. Stay here. I'll be right back. Dorian, close the door. Make yourself at home. I'm sure this will be a long night for all three of us."

Dorian hadn't expected Kelly to be at Lucy's when he showed up. He needed to talk to his other best friend to see if she knew Kelly was in town. Now, the answer to his question stared him in the face. Her eyes still held power over him. Knowing he should turn and flee, Dorian didn't move a muscle. He couldn't. Seeing Kelly in such a vulnerable state concerned him.

"Hey, you! Are you okay? Can I do anything to help?"

Is that a trick question? Yes, please!

"Hello, Dorian. I'll be fine in a minute. Panic attack."

"Oh, you still get those?"

That was an understatement. Kelly remembered her first one. She and Dorian strolled along the lake one night when she noticed

66

something moving in the water. Before she knew what was happening, dark shadows arose from the pitch-black currents. Her chest heaved, her breathing shortened, she froze in fear. Dorian tried to help but didn't know what to do or what was happening. Something else they never talked about.

"Kell, you, okay?" Dorian asked, snapping her back in time. "Did you hear what I said?"

"Yep, only now, they're heightened. Let's not worry about that. How are you? My mom told me what happened."

Dorian leaned against the wall, crossing one foot over the other. His biceps winked at Kelly. She looked at the floor to hide her rosy cheeks. *This man is too fine*, she thought.

"I was okay until I saw you this afternoon. Why didn't you tell me you were coming?"

"Are you serious? Dorian, we haven't talked in years."

"My number is the same. Always has been. You changed yours, remember."

Kelly didn't have any comeback. He was right. She had changed her number to start a new life. She knew it was wrong, but at the time, she didn't care about anyone or anything but herself. Her parents' divorce affected her in a bad way. Although she hadn't meant to take her emotions out on her favorite person, she had.

"Dorian, I'm sorry. I was young and stupid back then. My parents' divorce cut deep. I didn't want to take my pain and anger out of you, so I shut you out to protect you from me."

"Why? All you had to do was talk to me. I made a promise to you, Kelly. We made a promise to each other. You broke it."

"I know. You're right. I'm so sorry."

Tears fell down Kelly's face as she broke eye contact with Dorian. She didn't want to cry in front of him, but he was right. His words hurt. She'd lost her best friend and the boy she loved, now, he belonged to someone else.

"Here we go," Lucy said, handing Kelly a glass of water. "Did I miss something?" The looks on the faces of two of her favorite people spoke volumes.

"Lucy, I'm sorry. I should have called first. I'll go and let you ladies enjoy your night together. We can talk tomorrow."

"Dorian, don't go."

"No, don't go, D."

"You two should talk. I'll go into the kitchen and let you and Lucy speak in private. Don't mind me. I'm fine. Take your time."

Kelly stood up slowly. When the room didn't spin, she took that as a good sign and walked down the hall to the kitchen. She didn't bother looking back knowing Dorian's eyes were on her every move. She felt them upon her, immediately becoming aroused. *He belongs to someone else. Stop lusting after another woman's husband.*

"D, what's up?" Lucy pulled Dorian toward the living room, further away from the kitchen. "This isn't a good time. Kelly and I are in the middle of something."

"Luc, I apologize. I didn't mean to cause any trouble. I had to get out of that house. When I saw Kelly at Mack's, I thought my mind was playing a crude joke on me, but seeing her here, I'm glad to know I'm not crazy."

"That's up for debate, bruh."

"Haha…"

"Listen, Dorian. I know I should be sorry for not giving you a head's up about Kelly, but I found out a few hours ago when I went to get something to eat at Mack's. She's in town only because her plane made an emergency landing in Atlanta and her flight back to New York was canceled due to a storm. Otherwise, neither one of us would be seeing Kelly right now. I didn't tell her about Collin. She was in South America performing a dangerous surgery, so I made a wise decision to tell her at a later date. Her mother beat me to it. Don't be mad, but her being here, has nothing to do with you."

Dorian nodded. Relief washed over him, but so did sadness. Deep down, he'd hoped Kelly had come for him. She and Collin loved each other. He would want her here too.

"No need for all that, Luc. I get it. Thanks for letting me in. I know you're in a difficult predicament being as though you're both of our best friends. I won't hold it against you too long."

Lucy's mouth flew open. When she saw Dorian's face light up with laughter, she punched him in the arm. "Did you become a comedian in LA or something? You got jokes for days. Too bad they're not funny."

"Damn, that's cold!"

"What's so funny?" Kelly asked walking up the hallway from the kitchen to join them.

"Dorian thinks he is, but I beg to differ," Lucy exclaimed with a smirk.

"Wow!" Kelly responded trying to hide her amusement. The banter between them hadn't changed one bit, even though they hadn't spent time together in years.

"Kelly, you see how she does me? Take notice. It could be you next," Dorian replied, shaking his index finger at Lucy.

"She knows better," Kelly replied.

"Hey! No double-teaming," Lucy shouted. "You two always did like to gang up on me."

Kelly and Dorian hunched their shoulders with silly grins on their faces, which Lucy didn't find amusing in the least.

"SOOO...what are you ladies up to? Do you guys, mind if I hang a bit? I could really use a few friendly faces right now. I also need the distraction. My emotions are on overload."

Lucy and Kelly glanced at each other. They didn't mind. It would be good spending time together for old time's sake.

"Come on you two. Let's go find something to snack on in the kitchen. I have wine."

"Sounds good to me," Dorian and Kelly responded simultaneously.

~~~

That night, the three old friends laughed and talked until after midnight. Dorian left, while Lucy and Kelly sat up and reminisced about the good ol' days. At about eight o'clock in the morning, Katherine Bishop knocked on the front door with a delicious homemade breakfast.

Lucy put on a pot of Jamaican coffee as they ate. Kelly couldn't stop thinking about the man she still loved. She wondered if they would run into each other again before she left. She also wasn't looking forward to attending Collin's service and seeing Dorian with another woman.

"Did you finish the program for Collin's service last night?" Katherine inquired.

"We sure did. Would you like to see it?"

Before Katherine could answer, Lucy went into her home office to retrieve the document. She took pride in her work. Being a graphic designer provided Lucy with freedom and financial security. She loved what she did, and did it with joy. Her calendar stayed booked. For that, she was thankful.

Heading the folder to Katherine, Lucy picked up her mug and sipped her coffee. She needed it to start her day, and couldn't function without it. And being half Jamaican, Lucy didn't drink anything, but coffee shipped to her monthly by her relatives who still lived on the small island country.

Katherine opened the folder and her breath caught in her throat. "Oh my goodness, Lucy. This is beautiful. You are wonderful at what you do, my dear. Alice is going to love this so much."

"Thank you but I cannot take all the credit. Your daughter has a great eye for detail. Her ideas were fantastic. I simply followed her lead."

"You both are wonderful. Don't ever let anyone tell you differently," Katherine said with sadness in her voice.

"Mom, is everything okay? Where is this coming from? Did I miss something last night?"

Concerned about her mother, Kelly walked over and sat next to her. Lucy stood next to the island, giving them space.

"Oh, I'm fine, sweetheart. I'm just so proud of the both of you. Do you mind if I drop these off to Alice? We are going over to Collin's condo to clean up and pick out something for him to wear. Seeing him displayed in such a way will surely make this awful process easier somehow."

"Sure, Mom. Do you need or want us to help with anything?"

"Yes, Mrs. Katherine, we are here for anything you need."

"No, thank you. You have done more than enough. I'll see you both later for dinner. My treat. I'll call with details in a few hours. And I'm not taking no for an answer."

"Yes, Ma'am," Lucy and Kelly said. They watched Katherine gather her belongings and exit the house without another word spoken. A somber mood settled over them as they sat in silence thinking about what tomorrow would bring for not only the Carter family, but everyone who knew and loved Collin. Lake Lanier was yet again, riddled with melancholy and mystery.

Chapter 6

Gemma couldn't sleep without her husband lying next to her. When he left last night, after their walk, she wanted to go with him but knew he needed some alone time. Collin's death had taken its toll on him. The stress lines covering his handsome face and the tension she felt in his shoulders were clear indications of it. This week would be nonstop with the funeral and people in and out. Gemma didn't want to be insensitive, but she was ready to get back to their life.

Turning over in the middle of the night, noticing Dorian wasn't in bed, alarmed Gemma, especially since she'd seen someone from her past merely a few feet away from them, hours prior.

Shaking the thought, she went to search for him, hoping he'd come home. Knowing how close he and Lucy were, Gemma wouldn't be surprised if he'd spent the night at her house. She didn't t like her husband calling another woman his best friend, but she wasn't threatened by his relationship with Lucy. Their history didn't intimidate her, but Gemma wasn't a fool either. She knew from experience how best friends could turn into something more. It had nearly ruined her life.

She went downstairs to find Dorian asleep on the sofa. *Why hadn't he come upstairs to bed?* His brother's death wasn't a reason to pull away from her or stay out all night. She couldn't let that happen. Dorian wasn't the type of man to sleep anywhere other than with her, whenever they were under the same roof. He wouldn't start now, and definitely not in his mother's house. People talked, and Gemma wouldn't let her family be the blunt of conversation. The town of Lake Lanier was that way. She'd heard the rumors. Everyone has an opinion, especially pertaining to someone else's life.

Being a successful business executive and entrepreneur, Dorian traveled a lot. When they first got married, Gemma would travel with him. After having kids and starting her own consulting firm, she wasn't able to tag along as much as she'd liked. This kept their marriage fun and exciting, though. Their love life was healthy and happy, which both of them appreciated.

Gemma stared down at her handsome husband. He looked so peaceful. She didn't want to wake him, so she snuggled up next to him, covering them both with the woven blanket from the top of the sofa.

Dorian stirred. He sat up, looking around to remember where he was. He'd had one glass of wine too many with Lucy and Kelly before walking home. The good thing about being in a small town was that he didn't have to walk too far to get anywhere in particular. Yet, there are some things that go bump in the night in Lake Lanier.

Hearing the sounds of agony made Dorian remember why he left and never looked back.

Realizing he was in his mother's home, Dorian relaxed pulling Gemma closer to him. Her body felt good next to his. "Baby, why didn't you wake me up?" He nuzzled her neck with his lips.

"I didn't want to disturb you. I know you haven't gotten much rest lately. Lay down. Go back to sleep."

Dorian did as he was told, wrapping his arms tighter around his wife. Gemma smiled, drifting off into a peaceful night's slumber.

~~~

The smell of pancakes woke them the next morning as Alice cooked breakfast with her two grandchildren. Their laughter warmed Gemma and Dorian's heart as they listened closely, careful not to make a sound and disturb the outspoken trio.

"Grammy, may I add the chocolate chips this time," DJ asked.

"Yes, you may. Maysi, will you flip the pancakes for me?"

"Sure, Grammy. This is so much fun. We make pancakes at home with daddy all the time. I bet yours taste better than his."

"Of course they do. I taught your daddy how to make them," Alice chuckled.

"Hey, I heard that!" Dorian groaned unable to keep quiet any longer.

"Good morning, sleepyheads. You two should go upstairs so you can have some peace and quiet. I'll send DJ up to get you when breakfast to ready."

Before Dorian could say anything, Gemma placed her finger on his lips.

"Thanks, Mama A," she called out to Alice. "Babe, let them have their time. Come on, let's go get dressed."

Gemma and Dorian slipped upstairs to change. They made love in the shower before joining their family in the dining room for

breakfast. The entire time Dorian was with his wife, he thought of another. He felt horrible, yet, wondered what it would be like to make love to Kelly.

"How did you guys end up on my sofa?" Alice wanted to know as Dorian filled his plate. She didn't allow anyone to sleep on furniture that wasn't a bed. Dorian knew better.

"Uhm, I got home late and didn't want to wake anyone, so I sat down a minute to catch my breath. I guess I must have dozed off. Sorry, mom. It won't happen again."

"Did I miss something?" Gemma questioned, sipping orange juice.

"Dorian should have informed you that we don't sleep on sofas in this house. That's why we have beds. It isn't your fault, dear. You didn't know."

"Mama A, forgive us. I'll have your sofa cleaned before we leave."

"Oh no need for that, I'm sure you didn't do anything on my sofa that I would disprove of."

Dorian nearly choked on the forkful of chocolate chips pancakes he'd just popped into his mouth.

"No, Ma'am!" Gemma exclaimed. "We would never."

"I bet," Alice said, eyeing both of them like she knew a naughty secret about them.

"Mom, cut it out. Babe, she's messing with you. Don't pay any attention to her. Kids, how would you like to go to one of my favorite places today?"

"Yay!" they squealed with excitement.

"Okay, finish your breakfast and go upstairs and get dressed. Make sure to pack your backpacks with the things you need. We aren't taking the car."

"Are we going on a family adventure, daddy?" DJ asked.

"Yes, we are, son."

"Grammy, are you coming with us?"

"Not today, Maysi. Grammy has a few errands to run. I'll see you later and we can make dinner together. What would you two like to eat?"

"Grammy, I'm sure that anything you cook will be delicious," Maysi said. "Grandmothers are like that, you know."

"Like what, sweetheart?"

"You know, able to cook anything and make it scrumptious."

"Is that right," Alice said with joy in her heart." Her grandchildren gave her comfort in the midst of her storm of grief.

"Yes!" DJ and Maysi shouted.

"Why, thank you, very much! You two are more than a grandmother could ask for. For that, I am grateful. Now go do what your father said." Alice's heart was full.

"Yes ma'am," they called out running towards the staircase.

"Dorian, you and Gemma are raising my grandchildren to be wonderful people. Thank you."

"Mom, I'm teaching them what you taught me and Collin."

The mention of his brother's name caused Alice to freeze. She quickly turned her head and walked away from the table. She didn't want anyone to see her pain. Dorian immediately regretted saying anything about Collin in front of his mother. She was fragile. Truth be told, so was he.

"Mom! Mom, I'm sorry. I'm so sorry. Please, forgive me!"

Alice didn't bother acknowledging Dorian's declaration. She needed some fresh air and to be alone to gather herself.

"Leave her be, Dorian. She probably needs a minute. Let's finish up so we can get out of her hair a few hours," Gemma replied, pushing around the uneaten food on her plate. Suddenly, she'd lost her appetite.

"Okay," was all Dorian managed to say fighting back his own tears. He'd put his foot in his mouth big time. One thing he hated seeing more than anything was his mother upset. Getting up from the table, Dorian walked upstairs without saying another word. He was angry at Collin more than ever. How could his brother be so selfish? Why hadn't he talked to him about whatever was bothering him? They always talked. The last time they spoke, days ago, Collin assured him that he was okay. Dorian wished like hell that he had paid closer attention during their conversation.

"Daddy, are you okay?" DJ asked walking up to his father. Dorian lifted his son into his arms. "Daddy's a little bit sad right now son, but I'll be fine. Thank you for being a good boy for your mother and me as well as Grammy. I'm super proud of you."

"Daddy, did I look like Uncle Collin?"

Observing DJ closely, Dorian noticed for the first time just how much his son resembled his brother.

"Yes, you do, DJ. Your Uncle Collin was a handsome guy. He was smart and you remind me of him the older you get. He would have loved hanging out with you, son. Now, go ahead and finish getting ready. We are spending a fun-filled day at my favorite place."

"Okay, Daddy!"

Before DJ ran out of the room, he turned and ran back to his father. Reaching out to pull his face to his, Dorian leaned in closer. "Daddy, I love you. Don't be sad about Uncle Collin. He told me to tell you and Grammy that he's better now."

Dorian didn't know what to say. The air around him got thicker. Closing his eyes to focus on anything but his son's words, Dorian took a calming breathe and reopened his eyes. He stared at his son who released his face and ran off. An eerie feeling came over him.

"Babe, you good," Gemma questioned, walking over to grab her backpack. She was ready to get some fresh air and spend some

quality time with her family. When Dorian didn't
say anything, she paused and regarded him
carefully.

"Dorian, what's going on? You look paler
than popcorn without butter."

"It's nothing. DJ came to tell me how
much he loves me. That kid warms my heart with
his aura. How did we get so lucky?"

"We are blessed, babe. Now, get your stuff
so we can go. It's too beautiful a day to stay
inside."

"I'll be down in a minute. Is Maysi ready?"

"You know she is and waiting by the front
door. That's your child," Gemma replied pointing
at Dorian with a smile.

~~~

The walk to Pluto Beach—a hidden paradise—
not too far from Alice's property line, was a
breeze. The secluded trail made the kids feel like

they were on an adventure from one of the stories their parents read to them at bedtime.

"This is so cool, daddy!" Maysi yelled.

"Yes, daddy," DJ replied.

"How did you find this place, babe?" Gemma was impressed that such a small town possessed something so amazing. No wonder tourists flocked here to spend their summers and spring breaks, she thought.

"My father used to bring me and Collin here when we were kids. It was kinda our spot. I spent a lot of time here growing up and I wanted to share it with you all. Wait until we get there."

A few steps later, the Carter clan stood in awe, taking in the beauty of nature surrounding them. The white sand and turquoise blue water took their breaths away. A light wind danced through the trees as if welcoming them into their home.

"I have no words," Gemma managed to say with her mouth slightly agape.

Dorian smiled with glee. The reaction he'd gotten from his family was one he'd never forget.

"Come on. Let's find a spot under those trees over there and get settled in. We will be here a while. I hope that's okay, babe? I need this, especially today. Tomorrow, my life changes forever."

DJ and Maysi ran past their parents too excited. They couldn't wait to tell their Grammy about this place.

"Babe, you, okay?" Dorian asked Gemma who still hadn't moved an inch. Her beauty was astounding. The yellow bikini fit her to absolute perfection. Dorian couldn't take his eyes off her. Still, he imagined what it would be like in that moment with Kelly instead of Gemma. Shaking the thought, Dorian walked over to his wife and interlocked their hands.

"This place is wonderful. I feel like we're on vacation in the Caribbean. Thank you for bringing us here. It's nice to see one of the places you spent your childhood. I feel closer to you somehow."

Dorian lifted their hands bringing Gemma's hand to his lips. At that moment, he felt lucky to have her by his side. Nothing else mattered.

His gentle kiss made Gemma's heart, beat faster. She basked in the moment—their moment—embedding it in her soul. Then, she saw him, standing in the crystal-clear waters mocking her. Frightened, Gemma kept her composure, hoping it was her imagination playing a cruel joke on her. Closing her eyes, counting to twenty as her therapist suggested during one of these episodes, she exhaled a sigh of relief when no one was there.

"Come on. Follow me. This isn't all I want to show you, but let's wait. Let's enjoy our time with our children. Did you bring your camera?"

"You know I did. I never leave home without it." Clearing her throat, Gemma willed her fear away.

"Of course you don't," Dorian laughed.

In Gemma's spare time, she loved photography and was quite good at it. She offered a class at her consulting firm which filled up quickly once people saw her quality of work in person. Dorian was proud of her for following her dreams. He would do everything within his power to make sure she did. Someday soon, Gemma planned to display her work in a major art gallery in New York. She deserved it and Dorian couldn't wait to stand next to her as she received the recognition she'd worked hard for.

"Daddy! Mommy! Hurry up. We see a hidden path," Maysi called out. "Can we see where it goes?"

"Wait, honey. We have all day to explore. Don't you want to get in the water?"

Dorian wasn't ready to show his children his other secret but knew they wouldn't stop until he did. Looking at Gemma who had a look of curiosity on her face said it all.

"Thanks a lot, babe. Come on."

The short path led to a beautiful waterfall and hot springs. Dorian led the way, but nearly dropped to his knees when he saw Kelly in her red bikini sunbathing on one of the huge rocks. Inches away from her, was Lucy doing the same thing.

"Babe, what's wrong? Why did you stop?"

Before her husband could answer, Gemma saw the two women. She recognized Lucy but who was the other one.

Oh shit! Dorian thought, wanting to run and hide. *This is not how I wanted them to meet,* he deliberated still unable to take his eyes off of Kelly and her incredible body.

"Ahem," Gemma cleared her throat.

"Daddy, Lucy's here," DJ shouted, running over to embrace her.

"DJ don't disturb her," Maysi said, a few feet behind her brother. They adored Lucy.

This should be interesting, Lucy gathered, shooting a thoughtful look at her best friend.

Chapter 7

Kelly didn't know what to do or say. She covered herself with her towel when she noticed Dorian and what she assumed was his family standing there. The little boy hugging Lucy looked like a smaller version of him. She smiled and waved at the little boy and the little girl next to him.

"Who's she?" DJ asked, pointing at Kelly.

"That's Kelly," Lucy said. "She's my best friend."

"She's pretty. What are you doing here? This is my daddy's secret place."

"DJ," Maysi warned. "Don't be rude. I'm sure Lucy has a logical explanation as to why she and her friend are at Daddy's spot."

Lucy and Kelly glanced at each other. These kids were brilliant.

"DJ and Maysi, my friend and I have been coming here since we were kids. Your daddy included. He found out about this place from Kelly and me. He didn't know about the waterfall until we told him. But he did show us the beach that your grandfather showed to him and your uncle Collin."

Before Lucy could continue telling the kids about Kelly up walked Dorian and a pissed-off looking Gemma; the entire scene was quite amusing, but Lucy kept her laughter at bay.

"Hello, ladies," Dorian said. "What are you doing here?"

"That seems to be the question of the day," Kelly replied.

"I come here every weekend. That didn't change because you two moved away,"

Lucy said. "Hello, Gemma. Nice to see you again."

"Likewise. Kids, come on. Don't bother Lucy and her friend. Let's go back to the beach and make sandcastles."

"Okay, Mommy," DJ yelled, running toward Gemma. Maysi stood staring at Kelly. She'd never seen her before and was intrigued.

"Maysi, did you hear what I said? Get over here now!"

"Coming, Mommy. Lucy, nice to see you again and Kelly nice to have met you; I'm sure we shall see each other again soon," Maysi responded before joining her mother and brother who had moved back near the path tucked away in the trees.

"I look forward to it," Kelly called out.

"Yes, we'll leave you ladies be," Dorian responded in a nervous tone. "I'll bring them back another time. Sorry."

"Oh, no need for that. There's enough room here for everyone if you all want to stay.

Don't leave on our account," Lucy said. "You don't mind do you, Kelly?"

Kelly cut her a nasty look, but Lucy didn't care. This was a show she wanted to have a front view of. By the look on Dorian's face, Lucy saw that if he could have crawled under one of those big rocks and hide, he would have without a second thought.

"No, thank you. We are going back to the beach," Gemma answered before her husband could. Even though she didn't know the other woman, she knew actually who she was. *Kelly Bishop in the flesh,* she mused, taking in the sight of her. The behavior of her husband painted a vivid picture. He still cared about her very much.

Gemma wasn't an insecure or jealous woman, but she also wasn't naïve. The way her husband watched Kelly in her swimsuit was all she needed to see to realize he was attracted to her. She was gorgeous and her body was insanely fit. Gemma was tempted to remove her sarong and give Kelly a run for her money. But what would that prove?

Dorian was hers at the end of the day and he wasn't going anywhere. But still, in the back of her, Gemma wondered was there more to their story besides what she was told.

"No, thank you! We will catch you both later," Gemma said before disappearing into the hidden path.

Lucy and Kelly glanced at each other again without saying a word. They didn't want to make the situation more awkward than it was.

Waiting for Dorian and his family to get out of hearing range, Kelly couldn't shake the butterflies in her stomach. Why did being so close to Dorian affect her this way?

Last night after he left her and Lucy, Kelly couldn't stop thinking about him. She wanted to clear the air between them but on her own time. She didn't want anyone there but the two of them. What she had to say to Dorian Carter was personal. It wasn't anyone's business but theirs. Kelly knew too many people who put others in their personal business and wondered how it got out. Some things were better left unsaid or only to the person intended. She lived by that philosophy.

"Hey, you okay over there?"

Kelly regarded Lucy with a light giggle. "I'm fine. Today has been interesting but it's also been a great day with my best friend. How are you? Still, have that headache?"

Lucy didn't want to lie to her friend, but her headache wasn't from the wine they drank last night. They were more frequent and worse than ever. Knowing Kelly would be concerned Lucy decided to keep this from her until after Collin's funeral. Sure, Kelly would be upset but they would deal with that when the time came.

"It's a little better," Lucy said. "Today has helped. This place always makes me feel better. I'm glad you're here to enjoy it with me. We haven't been here together in a very long time."

"I know. I love this place. It's gotten me through a lot of rough times," Kelly admitted.

"Don't I know it," Lucy responded.

When Kelly found out about her parent's divorce, they'd spent many days and a few nights at the waterfall and hot spring. It was something about the warmth of the water that soothed the soul, casting all troubles and negativity away.

Word around Lake Lanier was that the mud in the water had magical healing powers—that the water contained minerals that produced positive energy and properties that helped fight cancer, anxiety, and other illnesses. Even if it were a myth, Kelly and Lucy spent hours in the water and smearing the mud all over their bodies.

There were also rumors about the lake being a burial ground of a burned city. Many claims have been made of seeing and experiencing supernatural phenomena in the town of Lake Lanier for decades. Kelly had witnessed it firsthand but refused to buy into the gossip.

"Hey, you want to talk about it?"

"Luc, I'm good. Seeing Dorian and his lovely family just confirmed to me that we weren't meant to be. Our time has passed. I wish him and his family all the best. Gemma is feisty, though."

"That's an understatement. I bet Dorian is feeling the breeze off of that one as we speak. There's something about her I don't trust. I cannot put my finger on it, but my gut has never failed me yet. Dorian needs to be careful with her, Kell."

"You're just being overprotective of him. He's our friend and we want the best for him. Tell me this, Luc. Have you really given Gemma a chance?"

Lucy took a deep breath. She didn't want to admit it but no, she hadn't. "I haven't if you must know. I cannot get close to her. My gut won't let me. I've tried."

"Try harder. For Dorian. If you don't want to lose him, you will. I can tell that Gemma isn't a woman to walk away from a fight. Knowing Dorian's best friends are women, she won't roll over and play dead when he attempts to put us over her. No woman should. Hell, I certainly wouldn't."

"I'll try, Kelly. I will, but I'm not making any promises to go out of my way. I love Dorian and he deserves happiness, but Gemma isn't the one for him. I'm a firm believer in just because we marry someone, that doesn't mean we always get it right. I wish them the best, though."

"Uhm, Lucy Jacobs, you are a very wise woman my friend. Don't ever change."

"Never."

"The sun is setting. Look. Have we been here all day?"

"We have and I love it!"

Lucy and Kelly took in the beautiful colors across the sky. Watching sunsets had become one of their favorite pastimes growing up that carried over into adulthood. Kelly wondered if Dorian was also admiring the beauty of the sunset—one they were both in close proximity of.

~~~

The day at the beach turned out to be great, Gemma acknowledged with joy in her heart. Dorian and the kids made castles in the sand, played Marco Polo in the water, and sunbathed without a care in the world. Gemma took it all in while she took picture after picture, capturing those precious moments in time forever. She joined her family on the sand, snuggling next to her husband.

"So, that's Kelly, huh," she asked.

"Yep, that's Kelly. I didn't even know she was in town."

The moment the lie escaped his lips, Dorian felt terrible but how could he tell his wife that he'd spent hours having a good time with his two female best friends last night? She wouldn't understand. Or would she? Dorian couldn't take the chance of telling her. He had enough to deal with this week.

"She's pretty. She also seems nice. What happened between you guys that your friendship ended? Why didn't you guys ever date?"

"Baby, can we not talk about this right now? I want to enjoy this time with my family before going back to face reality."

"If that's what you want, Dorian, but it's funny to me that you don't mention Kelly when you talk about your past. Knowing the three of you spent lots of time here as kids, is something I should know. Why is it a big secret? Am I missing something?"

Dorian sighed, sitting up. The sunset took his breath away, remembering when he, Kelly, and Lucy came to that very location to take in its' beauty every evening. He also couldn't stop thinking about the ones he and Kelly shared alone.

"Look, Babe. Isn't it wonderful?"

Gemma followed her husband's eyes. "Oh wow! And I thought California's sunsets were the best." She snapped a lot of pictures and then leaned her head unto her husband's shoulder. She could stay this way forever. Nothing else mattered. Maysi and DJ joined them and for the next few minutes, they enjoyed the sound of nature, while taking in the beautiful sunset at daddy's secret beach.

Chapter 8

"So, Alice, how are you holding up?" Katherine asked. "Don't tell me you're okay because this isn't an okay moment."

"Kat, I'm as good as I can be under the circumstances. This is hard, but I know that Collin isn't suffering anymore. I only wish I could have done more for him while he was here. He tried his best. God bless his heart. I'll miss him—that charm. I'll miss everything about him."

Katherine didn't know what to say so she wrapped her arm around her friend's waist and stood there in silence. They would stay that way until Alice was ready to go. All of the arrangements for Collin's service were complete. There was nothing more to do but wait. In two days, his body would be laid to rest.

"Okay, enough of all this sad business. I need to get home before my grandbabies get back. I promised the let them help me cook dinner. I have to stop at the grocery to pick up a few things."

"That sounds good. What are you making?"

"I thought about chicken and dumplings. I'm sure they'd get a kick out of making the dumplings."

"I'm sure they would too."

"Hey, would you like to join us?"

"Oh, Kelly's in town so we'll probably fix something quick and watch a movie or something. She leaves out tomorrow. I want to spend as much time as I can with her."

"Goodness. Why didn't you tell me she'd home? Now I know you have to join us. I, for one, would love to see her and I'm sure Dorian would too."

Katherine didn't say a word. She didn't want to upset Alice by telling her just how much she wanted her daughter to stay away from her son. Dorian was trouble for Kelly—trouble she didn't need in her life.

"Thanks for the invite but I politely decline. I will make sure Kelly comes to see you before she heads out. I will bring her myself. You enjoy your family, especially those grandbabies while you can. I'll be lucky if I ever get any with the way Kelly is going. That child doesn't want to let love, grab ahold of her for fear that she will end up like her father and me."

"Kat, I'm so sorry. Kelly is a smart and lovely young lady. She'll let someone catch her sooner than you think. Mark my words. I wish Dorian and she could have given love a chance, but we couldn't do it for them."

Katherine laughed. "No, we couldn't. My daughter is stubborn like her father. Once she makes up her mind, there's no changing it. I hope she doesn't miss out on something great because of it. He did."

"That he certainly did. His loss."

"Thanks. I still miss him, Alice. I miss him every day, but I'm learning to let go. Our friend Clarence is helping."

"Katherine Bishop, what are you not telling me? Did you finally accept his invitation to dinner?"

"I did. We did. And we plan on doing it again. I haven't told Kelly yet, so let's keep this between us for now."

"Sure. You can trust me. Kat, that's wonderful. Clarence is a great catch. His mother and my mother were first cousins. I've known him my whole life. You two are good for each other. And" Alice whispered, "You make a good-looking couple."

Katherine smiled from ear-to-ear, shaking her head in agreement. "Yes, we do! I like him a lot more than I want to admit out loud and to myself,

Alice. It's scary and intoxicating at the same time."

"Dating is hard. With the right person, it can be amazing. I keep telling myself that, Kat, although I haven't dated anyone since my husband passed. I do think it's time. I don't want to spend the days I have left, alone."

"Aww, Alice. You won't! There is someone great looking for you. Just watch. He's coming for you."

"I hope you're right, Kat."

~~~

The two friends went shopping and then parted ways right before dark. Katherine went home to wait on Kelly and Alice went home to wait on her family. When her grandbabies ran through the front door hollering and screaming her name, her heart was full.

"Grammy, we missed you so much today," DJ said, leaping up to jump into Alice's waiting arms.

"Yes, Grammy, you should have come with us," Maysi relished.

"Oh, sweethearts, Grammy missed you too. Something awful, I tell you! How was your day?"

"Our day was magical," Maysi delighted.

"What are we cooking for dinner, Grammy? We are starved." DJ asked, running into the kitchen full of energy. Gemma and Dorian shook their heads.

"Chicken and dumplings," Alice said proudly knowing hers was award worthy. "It's your daddy's favorite meal. I am teaching you how to make it tonight."

"Yay!" they shouted. Dorian couldn't contain the joy in his heart. He also couldn't wait to dig into his mother's delicious meal. Her chicken and dumplings brought instant comfort to his soul each time she made them.

"Need any more help, Mama A," Gemma wanted to know. If this meal was her husband's favorite, she wanted to know how to make it. She also wondered why she hadn't known this piece of valuable information before now.

"I'm going out for a walk," Dorian responded. He was out the door before anyone could stop him.

"Dinner will be ready in two hours so be your behind back inside this house by then."

"Yes, Mama!"

"I'm not playing with you, Dorian Carter," Alice said walking outside on the porch as she watched him son head away from the house. She wondered why he left instead of spending time with her. They would talk when he returned. Alice wondered if her son's behavior had anything to do with Kelly being in town. Her question was answered by her talkative grandchildren as they prepared dinner. They told her all about running into Lucy and Kelly, and the awesome time they had at the beach. Alice also noticed the tension in Gemma's face at the mention of Kelly's name.

~~~

Dorian found himself headed back to the beach, hoping to run into Kelly and Lucy before they left since he hadn't seen them leaving while he and his family were still there. There they were, sitting around a fire laughing like old times.

"We knew you would be back," Lucy shouted. "Might as well join us."

"Is that right?" Dorian hollered, heading in their direction. Kelly looked gorgeous as the shadows of the fire danced across her skin. His heart skipped a beat. Taking a seat next to her, Dorian leaned into her side pushing her gently.

"Hey you," he whispered.

"Hey, you," she whispered back.

"So, how did you get away from the fam? I know Mama A wasn't too happy seeing as though it's almost dinnertime," Lucy inquired.

"No, she wasn't. I needed some fresh air."

"And ended up here, right," Kelly teased. "You are so full of it, Dorian. You always do this."

"Do what?"

"Interrupt our girl time. You've done it since high school."

"Who me?" Dorian looked around pointing at himself.

"Yeah, you," Lucy and Kelly shouted. The trio of friends burst into laughter. When they heard movement in the distance, each of them stood up. Thinking it was probably Gemma, Dorian moved a few steps away from Kelly.

"Lucy? It's me," a familiar voice called out.

"Stevie Jones, is that you? What are you doing here? We didn't have plans tonight."

Kelly and Dorian looked at Lucy and then to Stevie. Where they, missing something?

"What's up Dorian? Man, it's good to see you. Kelly, hello again."

"Hey, man," Dorian said giving his once close friend a fist bump.

"Man, you guys haven't aged a day. I heard voices out here and had to come check it out."

"What are you doing out here?" Lucy questioned again, eyeing Stevie suspiciously.

"Hold up! Luc, what did you mean by your previous statement? You guys didn't have plans tonight," Kelly wanted to know.

"Never mind all that. Stevie has some explaining to do."

"As I said, I come here from time-to-time whenever I need to clear my head. This place has always done that for me. I also miss you guys. We should do better staying in touch. We were once really close. Why does that have to change now that we're adults? I miss my friends."

Kelly, Lucy, and Dorian glanced at each other.

"Okay, okay. If you must know, Stevie and I are kinda dating," Lucy said breaking the tension that settled over them. "Not that it's any of your business."

"What?" Dorian replied giving Stevie another fist bump. "That's great! I always knew you two had a thing for each other. What took you so long?"

"Please, let's not go there, D."

"Okay, Lucy. Chill out."

"That's what I thought."

"So, Stevie, come join us. Tell me and Dorian about you and my so-called best friend's relationship."

Kelly knew her statement was petty, but she didn't care. Lucy should have told her about dating Stevie. Supposedly, they didn't have any secrets among them.

"Kell, don't do that. I wanted to see if there was something before, I told you. Stevie, get over here and sit down."

"Damn!" Kelly and Dorian responded, amused at Lucy's bossiest and Stevie's obedience; their relationship was more serious than they thought.

"Hold up, woman. What did I tell you about trying to tell me what to do?"

Lucy didn't answer. She gave him a look and Stevie did as directed.

The now foursome, enjoyed each other's company catching up for lost times. Before Dorian could do anything, his watch buzzed. It was time for him to go. His mother wouldn't forgive him if he showed up late for dinner, and his stomach had growled a few times already signaling it needed food. Breakfast and lunch were long gone. It was time to eat. Lifting himself up, he said goodnight to his friends.

"D, man, before you go, what did Mama A cook?" Stevie asked. He missed her cooking. She was one of the best.

"Chicken and dumplings," Dorian said proudly, knowing all of them would envy him for the moment.

"Say, you think she'll be mad if I tag along for dinner?"

"Not at all, Stevie! Come on. She would be happy to have you. We cannot be late, though."

"Don't I know it," Stevie said, hopping to his feet.

"That's cold," Kelly and Lucy replied. "I guess we not invited, huh?"

Dorian looked at the ground with his hands inside his pockets. He wanted them to come but didn't know what was waiting for him back at the house. He knew Gemma wouldn't be too pleased with him if he showed up with Kelly in tow, especially with Lucy and Stevie. In his opinion, it did look funny, as he observed his surroundings. To anyone watching, it would appear as if two couples were on an intimate double-date. The beach of all places was a romantic setting if ever there was one.

"It's cool. We can make our own dinner, Lucy. I'm sure if we go back to my mother's house, she has likely cooked something delicious too. You guys go ahead. We'll catch you later. It was fun hanging with you all tonight. I've missed this."

"Let's meet up for lunch tomorrow," Stevie said.

"I can't," Kelly responded in a soft tone. "I leave for home tomorrow afternoon."

Dorian gave her a serious look. She couldn't leave. They hadn't talked yet. He wanted her to be there for his brother's funeral. Her presence comforted him in ways he couldn't explain but cherished. Kelly's energy did something to his soul. She was his soulmate. Instead of saying all those things out loud, he nodded and backed away from the group.

"Goodnight, ladies. Stevie, come on."

Without another word, both guys moved through the trees leaving Kelly and Lucy alone in the night. The sound of the waves crashing against the sand was tranquil. Nature's soundtrack played in the background, as the stars winked at the striking full moon.

Kelly noticed two shooting stars and quickly closed her eyes to make a wish.

"What did you wish for?"

"You know I can't tell you that, Luc."

"I know but it doesn't hurt to ask."

"You ready to go?"

"No, let's stay a little longer. You're leaving tomorrow and we probably won't see each other for a while. Our next trip isn't until six months from now."

A stillness settled over the two friends.

"Kell, can I ask you something?"

"Sure, Luc. Anything."

"Do you still love him?"

A lone tear slid down Kelly's cheek. Saying her feelings out loud, made them real and that was something she wasn't ready for yet. But Lucy was her best friend. She couldn't lie to or not tell her the truth.

"I've loved Dorian Carter most of my life. The feeling won't go away. I've tried. He's a part of me. He's embedded in my heart and my mind. I pray for him every day. I think of him every day. I long for him every day. But he belongs to someone else. Do I regret not telling him my feelings, absolutely? Will I ever express my feelings to him, probably not? Why, because I do not want to cause any trouble for him. Lucy, Dorian was it for me. Now, I have to move on somehow. Knowing that hurts like hell, I feel like a piece of me has died. Seeing them together broke my heart, but also, showed me what I'm missing in my life holding on to my past."

Lucy didn't know what to say. Her heart ached for her two best friends. One of them was being deceived and the other denied true love. She had to do something but what?

"Kelly, why did you wait so long? Why didn't you tell him? He went to see you. I know because I booked the flight on my credit card because he didn't have the money at the time. I swore I'd never tell you, but I was wrong not to. You both make me sick!"

"I was afraid. Watching my parents go from being madly in love to hating each other changed me, Lucy. I hated seeing them so unhappy—lonely inside their marriage. I promised myself I would never go through anything like that, so I closed off my heart to love. Even though Dorian had my heart, I locked it away. I would have ruined him, Luc. I would have ruined us. I couldn't let that happen. He deserved better."

"So did you, Kelly. You still do. You are a bright light in this dark world, Kelly Bishop. The love you have to give is incomparable. You, my friend, are an entire vibe! You are my real like Cristina Yang."

Kelly smiled through her tears. Leave it to Lucy to say all the right things when she needed to hear them most.

"I love you, Lucy Jacobs."

"I love you more, Dr. Kelly Bishop. Now get your behind over here and give me a hug."

They embraced a while before putting out the fire and clearing their mess.

"Let's go find something to eat and watch old movies," Kelly said.

"Lead the way."

Neither of them noticed the lurking eyes washing over them in the darkness. A shadow moved along the beach ready to reign terror over anyone in its' path. In the town of Lake Lanier, lost souls roamed about like fireflies. Tonight was no exception.

~~~

During dinner, Dorian was quiet, which alarmed Gemma and Alice. Alice knew her son.

She knew when something heavy weighed at him and wanted to do something to help.

"Mama A, these are still the best chicken and dumplings I've ever had," Stevie chimed in.

"Thank you, Stevie. I'm glad to see you and Dorian are catching up for old time's sake. You boys were together every day during high school. I almost charged your parents rent for you being here so much."

"You definitely should have, Mama A. I was here a lot."

"Even when I didn't want to you to be," Dorian whispered to Stevie, who chuckled.

"That's cold, man."

"I'm kidding."

"So, Stevie how did you and my husband meet?"

"That's a funny story." Stevie looked at Dorian for the go-ahead before sharing.

"It's cool," Dorian sighed, knowing Gemma would grill him about it in private later.

"Kelly and I used to walk to school together every day, until one day, I walk into the cafeteria and see Dorian sitting with her during lunch. I had a soft spot for her, but he didn't know and probably didn't care. She was the new girl in town, so most of the boys had a crush on Kelly. Anyway, they were in deep conversation about science and stuff I knew nothing about. I interrupted them with my jokes and the rest is history. Dorian helped me study and I taught him how to loosen up. Kelly challenged us in every area of our life. She was different than the other girls. Besides Lucy, none of them came close to being on Kelly's level. And not in a popular girl conceited way either. She taught us about the importance of having a personal relationship with God, how to study, how to dress for our personality, how to be a good friend, and all kinds of stuff most teenagers didn't care anything about."

"I see," Gemma retorted. "Sounds like this Kelly Bishop, is an amazing person."

"She is," Stevie boasted. He saw what Lucy warned him about regarding Gemma, wondering how Dorian ended up with her.

"I must get to know her better, considering she played such a huge role in my husband's life. Will you all excuse me?"

Gemma left the table. "Kids, come with me. It's time to get ready for bed."

"Do we have to?"

"Yes, do as your mother says, DJ," Dorian commented.

"Come on, DJ. Don't be a brat. Grammy, dinner was delicious. Thank you." Maysi said getting up to follow her mother. Before she headed upstairs, she turned to address their dinner guest. "Mr. Stevie, thank you for being my daddy's friend. He doesn't have too many and it gives me hope that he won't be alone if anything happened to us."

Stevie's mouth dropped as did Alice and Dorian's. Where did that come from?

KeKe Chanel

"Maysi, sweetheart, nothing is going to happen to you or your mom and brother. Why would you say that?"

"Just a feeling a have, Daddy. I'm sorry to have upset you, but you said to never keep our feelings inside."

Dorian walked over and pulled DJ and Maysi into his arms, squeezing them tightly. If anything happened to either of them, he wouldn't know what to do with himself.

"I love you both so very much. Go ahead. I'll come up to tuck you in shortly."

"Yes, Daddy," both kids replied.

Alice didn't know how to feel or what to say about Maysi's comment. Something didn't feel right. She began to pray silently. Stevie took her hand and bowed his head too. Alice couldn't lose any more people she loved, especially her grandchildren. The feeling she got when Stevie gripped her hand wasn't one of god. Keeping her thoughts to herself, Alice prayed harder—in her

127

prayer language—so that anyone or any ungodly thing among them wouldn't know.

Stevie thanked Mama A. for dinner, took his go-to plate, and walked out to the porch. Dorian followed him.

"Sorry about that, man. I don't know what's gotten into Gemma. She's usually the life of the party. Since we've gotten here, she hasn't been herself. I guess with Collin's death, it's finally becoming real the closer we get to his service. We did have a close relationship. Well, as close as anyone could."

"No need to apologize, D. We all have family drama. Take care of yourself and your kids. I'll see you tomorrow. Thanks again for letting me intrude on your family time. I missed it."

"Anytime, Stevie, you're always welcome. See you around."

Dorian stood on the porch until Stevie got out of sight. If he would have paid closer attention, he would have seen it hadn't been Stevie at all. The real Stevie Jones was working an overnight shift at the airport.

Chapter 9

Dorian didn't know what to think about Maysi's earlier statement as he lay next to Gemma fully awake. She moved closer to him, but he didn't want to be near her. Something didn't feel right. Being home, at his mother's house, showed how much he didn't know his wife at all. She was like a totally different person. At the mention of Kelly's name, Gemma changed right before his eyes and not in a good way. The confident, sexy, beautiful woman had become insecure, judgmental, and unpredictable.

"Baby, what's wrong? Why are you up?"

"Shh, go back to sleep, babe. I'm okay. I just have a lot of my mind that's all."

"You want to talk about it?"

Now, this sounded like the woman he'd married—so innocent and sweet. Dorian was confused.

"No, we can talk later. You rest. I'm going downstairs to get something to drink."

Gemma rolled to her stomach. "Okay, babe," she moaned. Dorian put on his sweats and t-shirt and went downstairs to find his mother sitting at the table reading her bible. She smiled when she looked up and saw him.

"Hey, baby. What are you doing up so late?"

"Can't sleep. What about you?"

"Can't sleep either. Is Gemma alright?"

"Sure, why do you ask?"

"She seemed a bit on edge at dinner. Did you two, talk about that?"

"No, she was already asleep when I got in bed. I didn't want to wake her. I know the past few days have been a lot on her and the kids. Once we return home, things will get back to normal."

Or at least I hope so, Dorian thought to himself.

"Oh, okay. Join me for some hot tea?"

"You have any cocoa instead?"

"Of course. Sit down. I'll make you some."

"Thanks, Mom. I can do it."

"I know but you like mine better."

Dorian smiled at his mother. She knew him better than he knew himself. He felt safe around her. They talked about everything for the first time in a long time. It was like old times—times Dorian had missed. He made a promise to his mother that he would do better staying in touch and coming to visit. Nothing would ever keep them apart again. Life was too short, and Dorian knew they needed each other now more than ever.

"Mom?"

"Yes, sweetheart?"

"I love you."

Alice gave a thoughtful look at her son. He seemed stressed, but she didn't want to pry. If Dorian wanted to share whatever it was bothering him with her, she would let it flow freely.

"I love you more, Dorian. Now, go get some rest. The next few days ahead of us will be demanding, which I'm not looking forward to."

"I know Mom. I know." Dorian stood up, leaned over, and kissed his mother's cheek. "Try not to stay up too late, Mom."

"I won't make any promises, but I'll try."

"Goodnight."

"Goodnight, sweetheart."

Chapter 10

Lucy and Kelly eat grilled salmon, rice, and veggies for dinner. They talked until Katherine came home from her date with Mr. Clarence in all smiles.

"I take it your date went well," Kelly asked. She wanted her mother to be happy and to have someone there in her absence.

Leaning back against the doorframe, Katherine didn't say a word. The kiss on her lips lingered, igniting flames in places she forgot she had. It felt good being admired by a man again—by a man who looked at her as if she were made of diamonds. Katherine walked across her open living room and joined the girls at the island in the kitchen.

"What have you ladies been into this evening?"

Picking up a cherry tomato off the top of the homemade salad, Katherine popped it into her mouth. It was said that eating tomatoes after a fabulous kiss would bring many more kisses and good fortune. Even though it was an old wives' tale, told to her by her mother and grandmother, Katherine believed it. She had to. She didn't want to lose hope of finding love again. Love is beautiful and Katherine missed having someone to give hers to.

"Mom, how was your date? From the look on your face and the sparkle in your eyes, it appears to have gone well."

"Yeah, Ms. Kat, look at you all smiling and stuff," Lucy teased.

"Oh girls, ladies don't kiss and tell. I'm turning in for the night. You two enjoy."

"Well damn!" Kelly murmured. Her mother didn't tell her anything. *She must really like 'ol Clarence.*

"Girl, your mother is a class act, Kell. I'm happy for her. So," Lucy got up from the stool and carried her empty plate over to the sink. "What movie shall we watch tonight?"

"It doesn't matter. You pick."

The faraway look on Kelly's face startled Lucy a bit. She wanted to ask what was wrong but didn't want to pry. Seeing Dorian and his family at the beach today must have been hard on Kelly. Spending time with him earlier also couldn't have been easy. Lucy knew how her best friend felt about Dorian. She also knew how he felt about Kelly.

"I'll be right back."

"Okay," Lucy said with a puzzled look.

Kelly went into her childhood bedroom and stood in front of the mirror next to her closet.

"Stop thinking about him, he belongs to someone else. Do yourself a favor and hold it together. You're out of here tomorrow," she coached herself. Taking a deep breath, Kelly returned to the living room to find Lucy and Dorian waiting on her like old times.

"What are you doing here?"

''Hello to you too."

His smile made her dizzy. How could it still have that effect on her after all these years?

Dorian couldn't believe he'd left his mother's house this late and walked to Kelly's. He had to get out of there. The energy felt off somehow, especially while Stevie was there during dinner. He wasn't acting like the Stevie Dorian once knew. The way he spoke reminded him of someone else, but he kept those thoughts to himself.

"Kell, I told Dorian we were about to watch a movie. Is it okay if he joins us? He looks like he needs a few friendly faces."

Kelly looked at Dorian and their eyes locked. It was electric. The chemistry between them frightened her. She'd never had a connection with anyone like the one she had with him. Like a current flowing through the ocean in search of the sea, Dorian sent waves of emotion through her.

"Kell," Lucy yelled, trying to get her attention.

"Huh, oh, I'm sorry. Yes, sure. He can join us. You guys want any popcorn?"

"Sounds good to me," Dorian and Lucy replied.

Dorian hid his smile. He'd felt the spark pass between them the moment their eyes locked. It excited him in a way he couldn't or didn't want to explain. All he knew was that he didn't want the feeling to go away any time soon.

"Need some help," he asked.

"No!" Kelly shouted without intention. "I can do it. You help Lucy select the movie. You know she doesn't always make the best choice."

"Right," Dorian agreed with a sly grin.

"Hey, I'm standing right here guys."

"We both love you dearly, but it's true."

"Whatever."

Katherine returned to grab a bottle of water from the frig. "Hello, Dorian. I didn't know you were coming. How's your mom? We haven't talked this evening."

"Hello, Ms. Kat. She's doing well. You know Mom. She's always the strong one for everyone."

Dorian lowered his eyes from Katherine, suddenly feeling overwhelmed with grief. The gesture didn't go unnoticed on all three ladies in the room. Their hearts ached for Dorian and his family. Losing a loved one was horrible, but losing someone so abruptly was a whole other story. They could only imagine how he felt. Collin was one of a kind. What made him do the unthinkable?

"Tell Alice I'll check on her tomorrow. You guys enjoy the movie. I'm kind of tired, so I'm going to bed."

"Goodnight, Mom. Sleep well."

"Yeah, goodnight, Ms. Kat," Dorian and Lucy said.

~~~

Lucy fell asleep during the movie. Serves them right for letting her pick. *Who the hell wanted to watch The Pianist?* Dorian thought.

"I told you not to let her pick," Kelly hissed to keep from waking Lucy.

"Hey, I tried. She insisted. We both know how persistent she is. You should have interjected. It's not my fault."

"Is too!"

"Stop it."

Kelly laughed despite the situation. She couldn't get the past hour and a half back that she'd wasted on watching this movie. The movie was brilliant but not what she'd wanted to watch tonight. They should have watched something action-packed or comical given the circumstances.

"Hey, can we talk, Kelly?"

"About what?"

"I think you know there's unfinished business between us that we need to address."

"Now?"

"Why not?"

"Shh, come with me. Don't wake up Lucy."

Dorian eased from the sofa and followed Kelly to the back patio. It was a pleasant night, and they would have some privacy to speak freely. Taking a seat on one of the chairs next to the pool, Dorian mimicked Kelly's action. The sky was full of stars. They gazed up into the universe, taking in the beauty of the night's azure for a while until Kelly broke the silence.

"So, what did you want to talk about? It's getting late and I know you have to go."

Dorian glanced at his watch. "I have some time. Are you trying to get rid of me, Kell? I'm not ready to go anywhere."

"Hey, I don't want to cause any trouble. Just looking out for you, is all. I could stay out here all night. It's peaceful and nighttime is my favorite time of day. But I think you know that."

"I remember. We've spent a lot of nights under these stars, Kelly. Remember when we almost got caught sneaking you back inside your house? Your mother is a true detective."

Kelly laughed. "Yes, I remember that night like yesterday. If you wouldn't have given yourself up, I would've gotten grounded for sure. Thanks."

"I'd do it again in a heartbeat to protect you, Kelly."

Sitting upright, Kelly fidgeted with her hands. Being this close to Dorian wasn't wise. She wanted to touch him, be closer to him.

"Dorian, why didn't you tell me you came to New York before now? Why didn't you let me know you were there?"

Sighing, Dorian rubbed his head, licking his full lips. Kelly gasped.

"I regret that decision every day. When I saw you with a guy, laughing and talking, I got jealous. I thought you'd moved on. I thought you'd forgotten about me. You changed your number, so I just assumed that he was the reason."

"What guy? There hasn't been a guy in my life, Dorian. Ever! I poured myself into my studies and work to keep from missing you too much. I'm sure my mother would have told your mother otherwise."

Damn, Dorian thought, listening to Kelly open up herself to him.

"D, you should have told me. There hasn't been anyone special in my life. When we lost touch, I was devastated. I didn't know how to fix it, so I focused on school and now my career."

"I didn't know that. My heart broke and I allowed anger and hurt to misguide my decision to leave without you even knowing I was there. I met Gemma the next day and jumped into a relationship without a second thought. Kelly, I thought I'd lost you."

Dorian's revelation pissed her off. *How dare he make assumptions about her life without her truth?* Kelly was furious. "Dorian, this is some straight-up bullshit! I thought our friendship was better than that. How dare you decide about my life without my permission? Hunter was a classmate, now colleague, who was there for me when I couldn't come home. We looked out for each other. He's from London, so he wasn't able to go home much either. He's also in a committed relationship with my friend Beth, who if you would have stuck around long enough, would have seen. I set them up because Beth and I were college roommates. They're engaged to be married this upcoming year."

"People make me sick using what they see instead of what's true to make rash decisions."

Dorian felt foolish. All this time, he'd been deceived, believing that Kelly had found someone else without ever giving him a chance when she assured him that she wasn't ready for a serious relationship. Now, he would never get the chance to be with her the way he'd always dreamt of.

"You know Dorian, until today, I didn't think you could ever disappoint me."

That statement stopped Dorian in his tracks. His entire body went numb. The one person he'd never wanted to upset was furious with him. He had to make things right again between them. He'd missed Kelly as a friend, and he didn't want to lose her again. Too much time had passed.

"Kelly, please forgive me. I cannot make any excuses and I take full accountability for my actions. I was wrong and I'm so sorry."

"Dorian, I don't know what to say to you right now. Maybe you should just go. We can talk later once this news dies down a bit. I'm mad at you, and I don't want to say or do anything that I'll regret tomorrow."

"I understand. I'll leave you for now, but we will talk more about this, Kelly."

"I don't see how. I leave tomorrow evening."

Getting up, Dorian reached over and pulled Kelly up with him. She didn't want to be next to him at that moment but didn't move away.

Resting his chin against her head, Dorian closed his eyes and inhaled the scent of her hair. It still smelled of fresh strawberries and lavender which had become two of his favorite fragrances. Before she pulled away, he wrapped his arms around her waist, drawing her into his chest. He felt her loosen up. Tilting her head upward to meet his, Dorian kissed her. To his surprise, Kelly kissed her back; at first, soft and sweet, then with lustful vigor. It was the most passionate kiss either of them had ever experienced—better than the one they'd shared on prom night all those years ago. It touched the depths of their souls. When the kiss ended, neither of them said a word. Dorian gently released her and walked out of the back gate.

Kelly stood there touching her lips. She knew exactly how her mother felt earlier, and she too would never tell a single person. When she made it back to the living room, Lucy was just waking up. She sat on the sofa and pretended to be fully engrossed in the movie that was coming to an end. Kelly smiled to herself. The kiss she and Dorian shared slowly melted her heart; yet saddened her because they couldn't be together. He belonged to another.

"Hey girl, are you okay?" Lucy asked, rubbing her eyes.

"I should be asking you that question. You fell asleep on the movie you selected, Lucy."

Lucy chuckled. "I guess I was tired. I'm sorry. Dorian left?"

"Yeah, a few minutes ago. He had to get home."

"Oh okay. I should go too. Let's do breakfast. I know you're leaving tomorrow evening, but I need more time with my best friend."

"It's a date," Kelly said still unable to stop thinking about the kiss she and Dorian shared moments ago in her mother's backyard. She walked Lucy to her car, watched her drive away, and went to shower and get into bed. Kelly knew her dreams would be filled with Dorian Carter.

Chapter 11

Gemma jumped when she opened her eyes, feeling the presence of someone. She wanted to scream for help but knew it wasn't wise. The person covered her mouth with his index finger as a warning. She nodded in compliance.

"Hi, baby! Did you miss me? I missed you. Why haven't you returned any of my calls? I know you saw me the other day. I hope you aren't trying to play me."

"No. I would never do that. What are you doing here? I thought we had a plan. Why aren't you sticking to it?"

"Plans change baby. Where are my kids? I miss them."

A knot formed in Gemma's throat. She

wanted to run away but something kept her from doing so. A powerful force settled over her, pinning her to the bed. Tears threatened to fall, but she willed them away. She couldn't show weakness in front of him. He'd use it against her like before.

"Please, don't do this! Not here. Not now. They're asleep. You shouldn't be here. He will be back soon."

"Oh, I'm not worried about Dorian. If he knows what's best for him, he will wake up before it's too late. You are toxic, Gemma yet I cannot get enough of you. Kiss me."

"Not here."

"Do as I say."

Gemma was then able to move. She pushed herself forward to the edge of the bed. The person standing in front of her smiled and knelt to his knees to become face-to-face with the woman he craved. Slowly, she tilted her head until she felt her mouth brush against his. When his tongue parted her lips, Gemma lost all voice of reasoning.

She gave in to the kiss, devouring her lover's mouth with heightened passion. A light moan escaped her, but she didn't care. She wanted him.

Pulling away, the man moved back from his forbidden fruit. Gemma was right. Now wasn't the time for them to get caught up in lust. They had a lifetime for that later if the plan worked the way that it should.

"Are you making any progress?"

"Yes! He doesn't suspect anything."

"Good. Keep it that way."

"I will."

Footsteps sounded in the hallway. Gemma's heart began to beat faster. She knew it was Dorian on his way back to bed.

"I'll see you soon, my queen."

Before Gemma could settle back into bed, Dorian burst through the door looking around.

"Babe, where you just talking to someone?"

Checking the bathroom in the bedroom, he flipped on light after light until he was sure no one was there but his wife.

"Who were you talking to, Gemma?"

The roar in Dorian's voice shook her to the core. She'd seen him upset but never in this capacity.

"I wasn't talking to anyone. You're hearing things, babe. I got up to use the bathroom and you came in the door just as I was getting back in bed. You're tired. Come to bed and get some rest."

Gemma glanced at the clock next to the bed, realizing it was well past midnight. Dorian had been downstairs for a long time—the same as he'd been the night before. *Had he been home at all?*

"We have a lot to do today according to your mother."

Dorian didn't flinch. Gemma was lying. He knew what he heard. Someone had been in the room with her while he was gone. He wondered had it been the children and went to check. Both were asleep in their own beds. His mother opened the door to her room.

"Dorian, what are you still doing up? Is everything okay? I heard loud voices and you know I don't tolerate that kind of behavior in my house."

"Yeah, mama, everything's fine. I'm sorry. Go back to bed. Goodnight."

Dorian didn't want to upset his mother by telling her someone had been in the house, so he kept that information to himself.

"Son don't tell me what to do in my house. What has gotten into you? Are you sure everything's okay?"

"Yes, Ma'am. Please, go back to bed."

"You go on back to bed. Goodnight. See you in the morning."

"Okay, Mom. Goodnight."

Heading downstairs to check things out to make sure no one was there, Dorian couldn't help but think of Kelly. He missed her lips. He missed her touch. He missed her.

The hidden shadow standing at the top of the stairs smirked in the darkness. Watching the scene play out in front of him was amusing, to say the least. His plan was working. Dorian Carter was slowly losing his mind. Soon, the life he should have had would be his. With the help of the woman he loved, his death would make all the things he wanted, come true.

But another shadow concealed in the dark corner of the Carter house watched, knowing it had to warn his brother somehow.

~~~

The next morning, everyone ate breakfast in silence. An uneasy aura hovered over them like a dark cloud.

"I'll see you all when I get back," Alice said before heading out of the house to meet Katherine. They had a few more things to do before Collin's service day after tomorrow. She didn't want to have his funeral on a Monday, but Alice also didn't want to hold his body longer than necessary. Anyone who wanted to be there would, no matter what day she had it.

"Bye, Grammy!"

"Love you, Grammy!'

DJ and Maysi finished up their breakfast, took their dishes to the sink, and ran upstairs to change. They were spending the day with Lucy and couldn't wait to start the adventure she had planned for them.

Dorian and Gemma looked back and forth at each other without saying a word. It wasn't like them not to communicate. For the first time ever, they'd slept with their backs to each other—both thinking of other people.

Gemma's guilt began to take flight. All this time, she'd never given a second thought to the plan she and her true love formed many years ago to trap Dorian. Yes, she loved Dorian but being in love with him, she wasn't. Gemma thought back to the day they met. She accidentally bumped into him, upset with the person she'd come to the party to confront about the problems they'd had in their relationship. Dorian, being a gentleman, tried to get her to smile by dancing with him. To her surprise, it worked. Gemma found herself dancing the night away with him, watching the love of her life grow jealous by the minute. Dorian was an amazing dancer. All the women there waited patiently to have their turn with him on the floor. Sadly for them, he didn't dance with anyone else that night but her. If looks could become daggers, Gemma wouldn't have died ten times over from the dirty ones she'd gotten.

When Dorian asked her out the next day when he called to check on her, Gemma didn't hesitate to accept his offer. She liked him. He treated her like a lady and made her laugh. And he was fine as hell with a smile that made her want to get naked. The more time spent with Dorian, the more Gemma liked him. It wasn't until the day they saw Kelly Bishop's picture on that billboard that she realized how much. That day was also the day a plan to trap Dorian was set in motion. A plan Gemma regretted going along with.

It wasn't until Dorian told her he wasn't from New York that Gemma realized she had somewhat fallen for him. They made sure to see each other as they dated long distance until Dorian asked her to move to LA to live with him. Gemma jumped at the opportunity. She needed a change. She and her ex drove cross-country, planning what they would do to Dorian Carter along the way. Gemma knew there was more to the story because why would someone be that jealous. Her ex was and hadn't let her forget it.

Gemma snapped out of her thoughts.

"Babe, what's up? Talk to me! This isn't us."

"When you decide to tell the truth, we'll talk. Until then, we have nothing to say to each other right now."

"That's not fair, babe. Think about it. Who would be in *your* mother's house, *late* at night, for me? Huh? Ask yourself that question."

Dorian thought for a minute, wondering if he was making something out of nothing. But he knew what he heard. Thinking about the mistake he'd made with Kelly, he decided to give Gemma the benefit of the doubt. She was the mother of his children and they deserved to grow up in a home with both parents. Depriving them of that wasn't an option.

"Listen. Let's spend the day together outside of the house. Mom is busy and the kids are hanging with Lucy. We have the whole day to ourselves. I want to show you where I'm from. Get dressed."

Gemma smiled an evil smile as she got up and went to her husband. Standing on her tiptoes, she grazed his lips with hers. There was no spark this time. Both of them noticed but shook the thought. Dorian exhaled. The kiss on his mind at that moment had happened last night. He wondered if

Kelly was thinking of him the way he was of her. Time would tell because he would make a point to see her before she left this evening.

"Are you sure? I don't want to be a nuisance. If you have plans, I can hang out here alone."

Gemma knew she wasn't fighting fair but what choice did she have? Dorian was changing right before her eyes since they'd gotten to his hometown. She couldn't put her finger on it, but it was strange to watch the man she loved, turn into a complete stranger. She also knew she should have ended the plan she formed years ago with her ex when she'd given away the other half of her heart to her husband, even though, she pretended not to. Deep down Gemma loved Dorian, but her ex wouldn't allow it. While he was still around, she and Dorian would never be happy.

"Babe, yes, I'm sure. Now go change, please."

"Okay." Gemma fought back her tears

as she headed upstairs to change. She was in too deep and there was nothing she could do about it now. If her secret ever got out, she would lose Dorian forever—she would lose everything.

~~~

Dorian.

Turning around when he heard his name called, Dorian nearly fell. No one was there. An eerie, yet, calming feeling settled over him. It reminded him of Collin. Gathering himself after taking a few minutes to calm his nerves, Dorian walked over to the sink and cleaned the dishes before placing them into the dishwasher. It was the least he could do to help out around the house for his mother. Since he and his family arrived, she'd made sure they ate three meals a day and homemade desserts in between.

Be careful, Dorian.

A plate shattered across the kitchen floor. Gemma came running to see if her husband was okay since she knew the children were in their rooms getting prepared to go when Lucy arrived.

"Dorian, baby, is everything okay. Are you alright?"

She looked at the broken glass on the floor and went to help clean it up.

"What happened?"

Still trying to process if his mind was playing him or was the voice he'd heard Collin's, Dorian didn't know how to react. He went to the broom closet and picked up the broom and dustpan.

"I'm fine. The plate slipped out of my hand. Let me get it. You don't have any shoes on. Stay still," he called out to Gemma.

After resting the broom and dustpan on one of the island stools, Dorian walked over to Gemma and lifted her off her feet. He wrapped his arm around her waist and carried her into the living room to keep her from cutting herself on the glass.

"Go get your shoes. I'll be done in a minute and then we can go. I'm good. The plate was wet and slipped. That's all."

Gemma didn't believe her husband but kept her thoughts to herself. The look on his face told her that something had scared him. Whatever it was must have been bad because Dorian didn't scare easily.

"If you say so," she mumbled in an annoyed tone. Gemma couldn't wait to get away from here. The moment they drove through Lake Lanier, she felt the disconnection among her and her husband.

Once they got out of the house and started their day together, Gemma and Dorian were their old selves. They laughed, played like children, and enjoyed one another's company. Lake Lanier was an amazing place, with hidden gems throughout. Gemma couldn't believe her eyes when she spotted a crystal shop. She loved stones and wanted to explore.

"Take your time," Dorian said. "I know this is your kind of place. I'll be right outside when you're ready."

"You aren't coming inside?"

"Nope, I can't."

"Why not?"

"I was banned from it when I was sixteen. Don't ask."

A puzzled look appeared across Gemma's face and then a smile. "What are you not saying, Mr. Carter?"

Before Dorian got a chance to respond to Gemma's question out walked old Mr. Benton, giving him an evil eye. The old man hadn't aged much. His demeanor the same—frigid and unapproachable; and his facial expression told that he wasn't too happy to see the young man on his premises.

"Hello, Mr. Benton. Nice to see you again, Sir," Dorian said, unsure of how the older gentleman would respond.

"Is it now? Wasn't it in our agreement not to get the police involved that you never set foot on my property?"

"Uhm, yes sir and I weren't planning on going inside. My wife loves stones and wants to look around your store. I brought her here, but I hadn't intended to break our agreement, sir."

Gemma regarding the old man and then watched her husband, something bad must have happened to keep him from going into the store with her. They loved shopping together.

"Babe, I don't have to look around if there's a problem. Let's go   !"

"Hold on, young lady. He isn't breaking any rules by standing outside. Come, let me show you around. You sure are one pretty lil thang, aren't you?"

"Hey, flirting with my wife is off-limits, Sir."

"Be quiet and mind ya manners. She doesn't know you as I do. And where's that other pretty lil thang you nearly destroyed my shop with? What was her name?"

The old man pondered a second before shouting out Kelly's name which by the look on her face, didn't go over too well with Gemma.

"Oh, so the plot thickens," Gemma said. "Tell me more about this incident, Mr. Benton. My husband seems to have a lot of stories involving Kelly Bishop. Only thing is, he won't share them with me."

"I'm sure," the old man snorted. "Those two were a match made in heaven. I, along with everyone else in this town thought they would surely end up together. No offense to you Miss, and if I do say so myself, he's one lucky man to have you as his wife. He isn't worthy. That's for sure. Come. I want to show you something. Follow me."

Gemma cut Dorian a wicked eye. She was tired of hearing stories about her husband and another woman from other people. Why was he keeping the nature of his and Kelly's relationship a secret? Hell, she couldn't judge him. She was doing the same thing.

Turns out, Mr. Benton's crystal shop was amazing in every sense of the word. Gemma was on a stone high when she finally met Dorian outside of the shop with several bags in tow. Mr. Benton had stones she'd searched years for and ordered a few he didn't have in stock.

"I take it you found a few things you like," Dorian teased, tilting his head to her bags.

"And then some," Gemma beamed. "Thank you for bringing me here, babe, but I think we should head back to your mom's. I don't want to carry these bags around and chance damaging my crystals."

"Sure. Let me carry them for you."

Gemma handed Dorian the bags and held his arm with her hand. It was good being close to him. The weather was perfect, and it felt like normal between them again. Hearing story after story from Mr. Benton about the adventures of Kelly and Dorian had turned out to be pleasant. It wasn't until she came face-to-face with Kelly Bishop that changed her mood.

"Hello, you two."

"Kelly. Funny seeing you here since you said you were leaving today," Gemma retorted.

"Hello, Gemma. Dorian, how are you guys? And to answer your question, my plane was delayed again so I'm here until further notice."

Kelly gave Dorian a thoughtful look but quickly turned her attention back to the woman questioning her motives for being in the place she called home. *How dare she?*

"Oh, I bet that sucks," Gemma remarked, in a sarcastic manner.

"No worries. I'm the surgeon so they wait for me."

Dorian turned his head to keep his smile hidden. The two women he cared about most, other than his mother, were bickering in sophisticated elegance, he wanted to watch for as long as they allowed.

"Looks like Dorian took you to Mr. Benton's."

"He did."

"Find anything good?"

"Lots."

"Okay." Kelly looked out to the side at the sparkling waters of the lake. Gemma's energy was toxic. She didn't want to be around her any longer than necessary. "Good to know. I'll check it out before I go meet Lucy for lunch. Nice seeing you two. I'm going to let you get back to your day. Next time you're in New York, look me up."

Dorian wanted to embrace Kelly but didn't. Peace in his home was better than the ache in his heart watching the woman he'd let get away turn and walk out of his life for a second time.

"We're going to have a talk with Lucy about letting our kids eat with a stranger," Gemma murmured. "They shouldn't be exposed to people they know nothing about."

"It's fine. I'll speak with Lucy when she drops them off, but there's no need for that. Kelly wouldn't harm an ant let alone our children."

"How do you know Dorian? You said you haven't seen her since high school. Am I missing something?"

"No, Gemma. But I've known Kelly for many years. She's a great person." *She used to be my person*, Dorian thought. "She's also a doctor. It's her job not to hurt people, especially children."

"You better hope so, Dorian."

"Of course."

Gemma rolled her eyes. She hated it when he said that.

Dorian turned and caught Kelly looking back in his direction. He knew then that he wasn't the only one still feeling the remnants of their kiss. He would see her later. He would make sure of it.

Chapter 12

Kelly lay in bed, rubbing her thigh back and forth, thoughts of Dorian clouding her mind. She couldn't stop thinking of him. Never in a million years would she ever think they'd see each other again, and here they were, in the same place at the same time—apart. She knew she shouldn't think of him this way, but Kelly couldn't help it. Dorian had her heart. She gave it to him when they were kids, but was too stubborn to realize and admit it. Fear does that—makes us think we're undeserving of love or the desires of our hearts. Kelly wasn't afraid anymore. Knowing love, experiencing the full power of it, was something she was ready for. Sadly, it couldn't be with the man she desired.

The sound of a rock hitting her windowpane startled Kelly. She stood up and grabbed the yellow baseball bat resting next to her bed as it had since she was eight years old when her father gave it to her on her birthday. She had an identical one at her home in New York.

Slowly pushing the curtain to the side, Kelly looked around. When she saw Dorian, her heart danced. Pointing her finger toward the back of the house, he nodded. This had been their routine since high school. He stuck out of his house and met Kelly at hers. They would sometimes meet Lucy and Stevie, or just go down to the beach and spend time alone. Tonight, though, neither of them wanted to chance being seen by anyone, so Kelly invited Dorian inside and to her old bedroom careful not to alert her mother. Without realizing it until she saw Dorian's eyes on her half-dressed body, Kelly reached for her robe to cover herself. She didn't want to mislead him in any way.

"Sorry," she said tying the belt.

"No need to apologize. You weren't expecting me."

"I wasn't but I also don't want to flaunt myself in front of you either. You are a married man, and we aren't kids anymore. Sit down. What are you doing here?"

"You have nothing to be ashamed of Kell. Your body is amazing. Always has been. I do remember how health-conscious you were back then. Good to know you haven't changed that aspect in your life."

"Thanks. I take being healthy quite seriously. We only get one body. We should take care of it so that it takes care of us. And you didn't answer my question."

"I had to see you, Kelly. I didn't want you to leave without us saying goodbye."

Kelly agreed.

"Thanks for showing my kids such a fun time today. They haven't stopped raving about spending time with a doctor since Lucy dropped them off."

"I'm sure their mother wasn't too pleased about that. I don't think she likes me very much."

Dorian smirked.

"No, she wasn't. They both laughed.

"Maysi and DJ are wonderful, smart, brilliant children. Their humor is astounding. I'm happy you have them, Dorian. I know they will keep you on your toes, so I won't worry about you too much."

"Haha," Dorian laughed. "They are special kids. I love them beyond words. I lucked up with those two and wouldn't trade them for anything."

"I don't blame you. They are very special."

Kelly got into her bed and covered herself with the comforter. She had gotten a bit chilly. Resting her back on the pile of pillows, she watched Dorian watch her. Their eyes flirted, holding a soulful conversation. Locked on each other, a spark formed between them—solidifying the bond they already had. As if their connection couldn't get any deeper, Dorian got up and walked over to join Kelly on the bed. Pulling back the covers, he slipped beside her. She didn't interject, wanting to be next to him. Their eyes never left each other.

Dorian slid his fingers into Kelly's, caressing the softness of her hand. She didn't pull away which he took as a good sign.

"Your fingers are cold."

"My fingers are always cold."

"I remember."

"Dorian, what are we doing?"

"Kelly don't ruin the moment, our moment. Be in it with me. If only for this night, I just want it to be you and me."

"This isn't right, Dorian."

"Then why does it feel like it?"

Kelly shook her head. She didn't have an answer to his question. Everything about that moment felt right, but they both knew otherwise.

"Come here."

She didn't protest, giving in to what she needed if only for one night.

Dorian wrapped his arm around Kelly's shoulder as she snuggled up closer to him, laying her head on his chest. She closed her eyes and captured the rhythm of the beat of his heart into her mind to preserve it there forever. If they couldn't be together, she would have some part of him in her memory.

"I've missed you every day, Kelly. I wanted to reach out to you on many occasions, but I was a coward. I was also young and foolish back then. I'm sorry."

"Don't do that. I should have stayed in touch. I never should have closed you out of my life, Dorian. That's on me. I let the fear of losing you keep me from giving us a chance. I regret that every day. I'll regret it always. The pain I saw my mother go through after the divorce from my father broke my heart and poisoned my mind against love."

"Shh, let's not worry about what could have been. Let's enjoy right now. People make mistakes, Kelly. We made a big one. No one's to blame. We were kids, trying to figure out life the best way we knew how."

No more words came from either of them for a while. They held each other, touching, caressing, basking in the moment—their moment.

An hour passed.

"Dorian, you should go. I don't want to cause any trouble in your life."

"I have time. And don't think any trouble in my life is because of you. I'm a big boy. I can handle it."

Sitting up, Kelly gazed into the eyes of the man she loved now more than ever. Without listening to her voice of reasoning, she kissed him. She kissed him with so much passion to make up for the time they'd missed. It was a soft, tender kiss that packed the punch of a thousand men, sending currents of desire to every part of Dorian's being. He felt it travel the distance of his body, hitting and feeding one emotion after another, forming several along the way.

Dorian returned the kiss with vigor, losing himself in the beauty of it. It wasn't until Kelly pushed away from him that he opened his eyes, knowing this would be the last kiss they shared. Not because he wanted it to, but because she wasn't his to kiss. She wasn't his to make love to. She wasn't his to love the way a man loved a woman. It wouldn't be fair to ask any more of her given the situation. And Gemma didn't deserve this behavior from him.

Dorian prided himself on being a man of honor—a faithful man who loved his wife and kids with every beat of his aching heart. He also loved Kelly. If letting her go once and for all was what he had to do, so be it. Dorian only hoped that she finds someone who would treat her the way she deserved and love her without compromise. It saddened him to think about another man giving her all of what he'd wanted to but what could he do about it now.

"Will you be, okay?

"What choice do I have, Kelly? How I feel doesn't matter. Are you going to be, okay?"

Dorian rested his head against hers in anguish. Never had he wanted someone so badly and couldn't have her.

"Dorian, can I ask you a serious question?"

Pulling back, he looked at Kelly. "Anything!"

"The kiss we shared on prom night, have you thought about it over the years?"

"Of course, at least twice a day and three times on the day it happened."

Kelly beamed with delight. She was also glad she wasn't the only one. "I do too. I also wondered how a life with you would be. I know it would have been beyond amazing."

"Yes, I'm certain of it," Dorian replied with a gentle smile.

"I go to work, come home to a lonely place, and all I want to do is share it with you. You're still my best friend, Dorian. Even though we haven't talked or seen each other in years, you have been the one thing that's constant in my life. I hope we can stay in touch. I miss my friend. Life has a funny way of showing you just how much someone means to you. It took me a while longer to come to terms with that. Had I known I would lose you, I would have done things differently."

"I promise, Kelly. You won't lose me again. That never should have happened. In a way, I don't think you ever did. We went down opposite paths. All along, we were bound to cross again. I'm just glad we were paying attention."

"Me too, Dorian, me too. What about your wife?"

"Gemma knows the meaning of friendship. It's one of the things I love about her. I know it'll take time for her to accept the fact that you will be a part of my life from this day forward, but she'll get there. It's not like we just met or anything. We grew up together. You two should have met a long time ago. That's on me."

"I hope so, Dorian. Existing in a world without you, knowing you're in it isn't something I want to get used to. It's no fun."

"Don't I know it," he responded with a gentle sigh.

A few minutes passed by without either of them saying a word. The energy between them intensified, and Kelly found herself kissing Dorian over and over. He let her, kissing her with the same intensity.

"I should go," Dorian finally said, standing up. Kelly stood with him, never letting him go. She also noticed the bulge in front of his jeans. Instead of moving away, she pressed her body into his.

"Not yet. I want to have you to myself a little while longer."

Wrapping his arms around her, Dorian and Kelly exhaled and held each other in a warm embrace. Before long, they swayed from side-to-side, their vibe—the soundtrack for the love generating between them. It was a beautiful song of unspoken lyrics, captivating their souls to last a lifetime and beyond. A perfect moment in time that neither one of them would ever forget.

Chapter 13

As Dorian walked home after leaving Kelly, he heard a noise in the distance knocking the silly grin off of his face. Sure it was only animals playing in the night; he didn't pay much attention to it. The closer he got to the hidden beach, the louder the noise became. Dorian went through the bushes to check it out. That way was the shortcut he took home now that his mother lived where she did.

The beach looked magnificent that night—the water strumming back and forth on the sand, creating a peaceful atmosphere. Dorian stood, taking in the sereneness. Suddenly, a chill ran through him. He shuttered, blowing his breath into his hands. It was strange given the temperature outside was pleasant in Lake Lanier this time of year.

"I should get home," he said aloud to no one. As much as he wanted to stay on the beach and bask in the night, he knew his mother would wait up for him.

Dorian, help me!

"Hello, is someone there?" Dorian turned from side to side to see if anyone was there.

Brother, I need your help. Don't let them take me.

"Collin? Is that you? Where are you? Don't let who take you? Hello!"

Dorian couldn't believe his ears. *I must be going insane.*

"No, you're not, brother. It's me."

Suddenly, as if appearing out of nowhere, Collin stepped into the light so Dorian could see him. He looked afraid, sad, in disarray—nothing like his self.

"Collin, how are you here? How is this possible? What are you doing here? What's happening?"

"Dorian, stop with the questions, bro, I don't have much time. Listen, I need you to go to my condo and get something for me."

Collin looked behind him as if someone or something was coming. Dorian could tell his brother was afraid of whatever it was. He moved his head to look around Collin to see if someone was there. Total darkness greeted him.

"Focus, D, this is important to where I end up when I transition."

"I am, Collin. Mom and Mrs. Kat went to your place yesterday. I think they cleaned it out."

"No, I made sure they didn't. I need you to go there. I hid something there that explains everything. I want you and Mama to know why this happened and how. I need you to do this before I can move on. I'm stuck. I'm afraid. I don't want to be here anymore, D. They're after me and I'm tired of running."

"Collin, this is insane. Who's after you? I will protect you."

The look on Collin's face said it all. Dorian hadn't protected his brother while he was alive so how would he do so now?

"Listen, D, I know how it looks and sounds, but I was given a day to come back and get help. That's all I have. I need you to do this for me, please! Time is running down."

"Of course, I'll help you, Collin. Tell me what I have to do."

~~~

When Dorian got home that night, his mother was up just as he thought. She smiled at him when he walked into the kitchen to join her. "Hey, baby. How was your walk?"

"Hi, Mama. It was nice. There's a lot on my mind. I needed some time alone to process my feelings. Collin's death doesn't feel real, even though I know it is."

Alice considered her son with a thoughtful look, but didn't have the words to comfort him. She was dealing with her own feelings and emotions. Losing a child should never feel normal. After a few minutes, Alice finally spoke.

"You deserve to have some alone time, Dorian. It isn't healthy for anyone to neglect their mental energy to please someone else. Remember to always take care of you, Dorian. Promise me."

Dorian nodded.

"Your wife came down about thirty minutes ago looking for you. I told her you went for a walk. I hope I didn't lie."

"Mom, you told her correctly. I think I'm going to go to Collin's place in the morning. I want to make sure it's packed up and see if he has anything I want if that's okay."

"Sure, when Katherine and I went over there the other day, I didn't have it in me to do everything in one day. I wasn't ready to let go and say goodbye. You want me to come with you?"

"No, Ma'am. I would love going alone. I'll be back in plenty of enough time for the service, so don't worry."

"I'm not worried. I know you won't be late for your only brother's funeral. I also know you would never upset your mother like that either."

"Of course not," Dorian said walking around to kiss his mother on the forehead. "Goodnight. See you in the morning."

"Goodnight."

"Don't stay up too late, okay."

"I won't. I'll be up in a few. I want to finish up this chapter first."

"Okay."

Dorian smiled at his mother, knowing he'd miss her so much when he left. He thought about Gemma's offer, deciding to speak with her after the service about coming to live with them. He had to try, although he knew she wouldn't.

When Dorian got to the room he shared with his wife, he noticed she wasn't there. Checking on the kids, he saw she wasn't with them either. *Where was she? Had she gone out to search for him?*

Dorian's thoughts went back to last night when he was sure he'd heard another voice in the room with Gemma. She was hiding something or was it more like someone? He would get to the bottom of it, but tonight, he didn't have the will or desire. The only person on his mind was Collin. His brother needed his help and in order to do it, Dorian had to remain focused.

Chapter 14

Lucy and Stevie's date turned out to be sweet, although it was later than usual. His working late that night prevented them from meeting earlier, so Lucy was able to spend time with Lucy and Dorian.

She and Stevie had a lot in common which they both found refreshing. After their high school graduation, Stevie moved to Atlanta for school, and they sort of lost touch the same way Kelly and Dorian had. Since his mother passed, he came home every weekend to check on his father. Lucy loved that about Stevie, how he valued family. She could see herself starting something serious with Stevie and it frightened her in a good way.

"So, when can we do this again," Stevie asked?

"When will you be back?"

"I'll be back next weekend and I hope to spend some time with you Lucy. I like you a lot. Truth be told, I've liked you since we were teenagers."

"How come you never said anything?"

"Because I thought you had a thing for Dorian. All the girls did. I just assumed you were one of them too."

"Well, we all know what happens when we assume," Lucy teased, giving Stevie a playful punch on the shoulder.

"I didn't want to cause any problems within our group. I enjoyed hanging out with you guys. When I found out about Dorian and Kelly, I'd moved to Atlanta. What you think will happen with those two?"

"Who knows, but he's married."

"It's kinda sad if you ask me. Desiring someone for so long and never getting the chance to be with them in the way you want. I hope whatever's supposed to happen, happens in their favor."

"Me too," Lucy said as she got out of Stevie's car.

Lucy noticed Gemma walking hand in hand with a shadowy figure of a man, approaching her house. About to call out to them, thinking the man was Dorian, Lucy paused when she caught a glimpse of the red eyes next to Gemma. It definitely wasn't Dorian. But who or what was it? The rumors of Lake Lanier hit Lucy like a tidal wave. She didn't believe in the things she heard, but lately, she was beginning to think otherwise.

"Holy shit! Did you see that," Stevie shouted?

"Yes. Who is that with her? Those eyes don't belong to any human, that I'm sure of," Lucy replied in a whisper.

191

"Damn   right!"   Stevie   agreed. "What should we do?"

"Follow them?"

Stevie hunched his shoulders. Lucy did the same. She jumped back into the passenger's side of his car, scooting down so she wasn't seen. She demanded Stevie do the same which he did without question.

"You think she saw us?"

"I don't know."

"What should we do, Stevie?"

"We owe it to Dorian to find out, Luc."

Before Stevie could put the car in reverse, Gemma hit the window on Lucy's side. They both nearly jumped out of their skin in horror, screaming.

"What are you guys doing?" Gemma yelled.

Cracking the window slightly, Lucy put on a brave front, but fear soared throughout her entire body.

"Don't let it down any further," Stevie murmured. "I don't trust her."

Lucy agreed.

"Gemma, what are you doing out here? Where's Dorian? Did he go on home?"

"What are you talking about? Dorian isn't with me. I came to see if he was with you. Obviously not," Gemma said. "Sorry if I interrupted anything. See you both tomorrow at the service."

Stevie through up his hands in a waving motion, but didn't say a word. He knew what they'd seen. Gemma was a strange woman. Dorian didn't know who he had as a wife in his opinion, but he planned to tell him.

"That was weird as hell, Luc."

"I know," she responded slightly out of breath. "Stevie, I know you've heard the stories about Lake Lanier. Do you believe them?"

Stevie pondered for a moment trying to figure out the best way to tell Lucy he did believe the stories. He'd seen firsthand the supernatural activity in their small town. People came from all around to witness the accounts for themselves. Working at the airport afforded Stevie the opportunity to hear many tales—good and bad—on the history of Lake Lanier.

"Lucy, what I'm about to share with you is some spooky shit. My father told me, but I didn't believe him until I came face-to-face with it many years ago."

Lucy listened with anticipation, feeling her body tighten. She wanted to hear what Stevie had to say but also wanted to flee to her house and stay there forever. Those red eyes gave her chills.

"Some time ago, the town of Lake Lanier was a thriving town. Legend has it that the lake was formed by flooding surrounding communities. One of the communities had a cemetery said to be cursed by the dead. It's been said that the souls of the people from the cemetery are evil. Many people have died on the lake or claimed to have seem ghosts underneath the water. My dad and I were fishing one day when I were around 9 years old when we noticed a woman sitting along the banks of the lake. We called out to her to see if she needed help, but she

didn't seem to see or hear us. Next thing we know, she's gone. Like disappeared right before our eyes, Lucy. After that, from time to time, we would see her all around town and at the lake."

Silence washed over the car as Lucy processed what Stevie told her. Now all the mysterious deaths in the lake begin to make sense. She no longer wanted to talk about it.

"So, how was dinner with the Carter family? Did Mama A. enjoy seeing you?"

Stevie gave Lucy a questioning look. "What are you talking about, Lucy? I was at work until I called you."

Lucy gripped her right arm and squeezed. How hadn't she caught that. She knew Stevie was working, but seeing him at the beach, she assumed he'd gotten off early.

Turning to face him in the car, Lucy shook her head back and forth in disbelief. What she was about to say out loud would change everything for the people she cared for most and herself.

"Stevie, we thought it was you at the beach with us. You left with Dorian to join his family for dinner. This shit is crazy. Who was it if it wasn't you?"

"Shit!" Stevie rubbed his face and rested his hands on the top of his head. "Lucy, I wish it were me, but I promise you, I was at work. Whatever it is, isn't human. I think it's time to face reality and also tell Dorian and Kelly before someone gets hurt."

"I'm afraid Stevie. You should go. We can discuss what we'll do tomorrow. It's late, I'm tired, and the shit we just saw has me on edge."

"Do you want me to stay a while until you calm down?"

"No. I'll be fine. You've had a long day. Please be careful and can you let me know you made it home safely?"

"Of course I will. Lucy Jacobs, I like you a lot. Don't let anything happen to you, please."

"You too!"

Lucy waited a few minutes before she opened

the car door and ran into her house.

Stevie waited before driving off to make sure Lucy was safely inside. He didn't want any funny business, considering what they'd just seen. Something evil was among them—something he'd seen before—the same day Dorian and his family came to town.

As Stevie drove away, Lucy's heart fluttered while she watched him. He waved and honked his horn before heading in the opposite direction of Gemma. It was the last time anyone saw him. His truck was found a week later at the bottom of the lake, but his body was never recovered.

Chapter 15

The day of Collin's funeral was a sad and gloomy day. A melancholy mood settled over the town of Lake Lanier, mourning the loss of their beloved son. Despite his struggles, Collin was loved by all who knew him. He would be greatly missed.

Alice and the kids gathered into the funeral car, waiting on Dorian, Gemma, and Lucy. They stood on the porch for a break in the rain. Dorian couldn't stop thinking about his encounter with Collin at the beach and Lucy couldn't stop thinking about what she'd seen either. At first, she and Stevie thought Gemma was with Dorian, but when they realized it wasn't him, Lucy knew she had to say something. She decided to wait until after Collin's service when everyone left for home. Her best friend deserved to know the kind of woman he married. Lucy wished they would have told Dorian that night like Stevie wanted to, but there was nothing she could do about that now. She wished Kelly was there to help her decide. Kelly was the rational one. Always had been except for when it came to her love life.

Last night, after Stevie drove away, Lucy immediately called to tell Kelly what they saw. Her best friend was supportive as usual, but agreed with her about waiting until after the funeral. The Carter family was dealing with enough. This wouldn't help.

Lucy thought Stevie would meet them at the house and they all go to the church together, but he must have gone straight there instead. He never let her know if he made it home safely last night. When she called him this morning, he hadn't answered or returned her call. Lucy tried not to worry, but she couldn't shake the thought that he was in trouble.

"We should go," Dorian said. "You two take the umbrella. I'll make a run for it.

"Okay," Gemma replied.

Lucy nodded. Her mind was stuck on Stevie. A powerful feeling of terror engulfed her. She caught the railing on the steps to keep from falling down them into the rain. At that moment, she felt as if something terrible had happened to him. Lucy pushed herself to get to the car. Her heart ached.

During the short ride to the church, Lucy bounced her leg. Maysi taught her knee, giving her a thoughtful look.

"Aunt Lucy, are you okay? You don't look so well."

"Maysi, I'm fine. Don't worry."

Lucy gripped the little girl's hand, squeezing it gently to reassure her and herself that her statement to Maysi was true. Fact of the matter was Lucy didn't know whether to panic or mourn.

Today still didn't make any sense to her. Collin wasn't the type to end his own life.

Maysi leaned over to get closer to Lucy. Something in the way she did made everyone look at her with concern.

"Sweetheart is everything alright," Dorian asked?

When she didn't say anything, Lucy put her arm around her. It wasn't like Maysi to be this quiet.

"Maysi, you want to talk about whatever it is that's bothering you, honey?"

Gemma took in the scene, wanting to intervene but knew everyone would find it suspicious.

"Aunt Lucy, I'm okay. Really! I'll be much better when we get out of this car. It smells weird."

Everyone laughed. Maysi had a point. The car did somehow smell funny kinda like rotten eggs.

"DJ, you okay, buddy?" Gemma questioned.

He didn't look at her or say a word. DJ tucked his head into his grandmother's side and closed his eyes.

"Ah, baby, you didn't get enough sleep last night?"

"No, Grammy. I didn't. I was too afraid to sleep."

"Why, sweetheart, there's nothing in Grammy's house to be afraid of."

"I wish that were true," DJ whispered for only Alice to hear. She wondered if there was something she should worry about. After they got back home, she would talk to him in private to see what he had to say.

"Oh, Mama A, DJ is being dramatic. He didn't go to bed when I told him to and now, he's placing blame on anything when he should take responsibility for his actions of defying his mother. That's what happens when children disobey their parents. I told you and Maysi to go to sleep, but I'm sure you both talked and laughed and whatever is it you do in that room all night. Sit up straight before you wrinkle your clothes," Gemma said an octave higher than necessary. The adults in the car gave her a look, letting her know to back off.

"Go ahead, take his side. That doesn't change the fact that he's whiny and sleepy. Next time, I bet he'll go to sleep. Look," she pointed. "We're here."

Gemma opened the car door before the car stopped rolling. Dorian didn't know what to say. She'd never spoken to DJ in that manner. He didn't like it one bit. And from the look on his mother's face, neither did she.

"What's gotten into your wife, Dorian?"

"Mama, let me handle it. Don't say anything to her, please."

"You had better before I do. She doesn't talk to my grandchildren in that tone, ever. I know she's their mother and I respect that, but the way she lit into DJ was uncalled for. I've never gotten involved in your marriage or parenting skills. Don't make me!"

"I know, Mama. I'll take care of it. Trust me."

"I do trust you, Dorian. I hope by the end of the day, I won't come to regret it.

Alice gave her son a disgusted look, but kept her mouth shut. Her grandbabies were listening. Besides, it wasn't the time or place to get into a heated argument, which was sure to ensue if they didn't put a halt in their conversation.

"You won't, Mama. Come on, it's almost time."

Dorian didn't want to be where he was. The note he'd found in Collin's apartment told him that his brother was battling more demons than they ever realized. But the way he described the demon after him, hit close to home. Dorian recalled DJ and Maysi speaking of a red eyed monster in their house before they came to Lake Lanier. Was it the same demon Collin wrote about in his note?

"Dorian, hey, are you coming," Lucy asked, tapping his arm to get his attention.

"I'm right behind you, Luc. Is Kelly coming?"

Lucy felt terrible. She'd forgotten to mention that Kelly left earlier that morning. The weather cleared up enough for her plane to make the flight, and the surgery she was to perform couldn't wait any longer.

"D, she left this morning. She wanted to be here, but duty calls. I'm sorry I didn't tell you sooner."

Dorian's heart hankered, hearing Kelly wouldn't be there when he needed to have her there. Her presence would make all the difference, even though he wanted more of her. Plus, Collin would want her to be there. They were still friends according to the note which Dorian hadn't known over the years because his brother sure hadn't mentioned it.

"It's okay. I know she can't put her life on hold for me. I hate I didn't get a chance to say goodbye."

"She gave me this to give to you," Lucy replied, handing over a folded piece of paper from her dress pocket. Dorian took it, placing it inside his jacket. He wanted to read it right away, but knew it wasn't the time.

"Thanks, Luc. Let's go. Everyone's waiting."

Collin's service was beautiful. Everyone said amazing words about him. Dorian fought back his tears for as long as he could, but when Maysi got up from her seat and walked up to the podium when the pastor asked did anyone else want to say a few words about Collin, Dorian lost it. The way she spoke of her uncle—the uncle she hadn't seen on a regular basis—everyone dabbed at their eyes.

"Uncle Collin was a great friend. He would call my brother and me on our birthdays, for Christmas and sometimes just because. He loved to sing. I don't think anyone knew that about

Uncle Collin, but he did, and he was good at it. He was the most caring man I know besides my Daddy. I'll miss my Uncle Collin, but I know he's safe now."

Maysi's words touched everyone in the church that day, but also, raised suspicions too. She spoke like a professional, so poised and purposeful. Alice beamed with joy watching her granddaughter speak about her Collin in such a graceful way—in a way she hadn't known him. It gave her peace. But what had her granddaughter meant by her last comment?

~~~

Back at the house, people gathered around talking, eating, and enjoying fellowshipping with each other. Alice entertained her guests in true Carter form, Katherine right by her side. Lucy made sure to go around the house cleaning up anything that didn't belong, fetch drinks, or replenish food orders. She felt like a maid, but didn't mind doing it. Alice and Dorian were her family. She busied herself to keep from overthinking about the fact that Stevie hadn't been at the church or come back to the house.

Lucy knew without a doubt something terrible was the only possible explanation to why he wasn't there. Dorian noticed too, thinking the same thing.

"We need to talk," he said, pulling Lucy along with him to the back of the house. A few empty cups fell to the floor. "Leave them. We will come back and clean up."

"Okay!"

A few people eyed Dorian and Lucy with inquisitive eyes along the way, but they didn't acknowledge them. They had more important things to attend to. The looks were also something they'd gotten used to. People in Lake Lanier just assumed Lucy and Dorian had a thing going on when they were teenagers, especially when he and Kelly never got together.

"Stop running in the house!" They heard Alice shout.

"Yes, Ma'am!"

When Dorian was sure the coast was clear, he let go of Lucy's hand, pacing back and forth.

"What's wrong, D?"

"Luc, I don't know where to start. You may not believe me, anyway."

"Try me," she said, giving Dorian her undivided attention.

Dorian rubbed his chin, releasing a breath before he told Lucy about Collin.

"The other night as I walked home, I heard a voice coming from our beach. I went to check it out and you will never guess what I saw."

Lucy didn't say a word.

Dorian continued.

"Collin. Lucy, Collin appeared out of nowhere. He walked right up to me. I nearly ran scared, but I manned up. I stood there and talked to my dead brother."

Lucy covered her mouth to conceal her squeal. They didn't need anyone coming from the front to interrupt their conversation.

"What did he say?"

"He said he needed my help, that something was after him trying to keep him from crossing over to the other side. Lucy, up until that moment, I hadn't given much thought to what happens to us when we die. Honestly, I didn't care to think about it. Collin asked me to go to his condo and look for something he left there that would explain what happened to him and why."

"Did you?"

Dorian removed his wallet from his back pocket and opened it. He pulled out a piece of paper like the one Lucy gave him and handed it over to her. She looked at the paper and then back to Dorian for answers. When he shook the paper for her to take it, Lucy did with a shaking hand. Unhurriedly, she unfolded the paper and glanced at it with wide eyes.

A few seconds passed before Lucy looked at Dorian with a face full of shock.

"Dorian, I don't know what to say. What are you going to do? How can I help?"

"I don't know. This is serious, Lucy. Someone taunted my brother to death. He took his own life to be free from the mental turmoil he was experiencing all these years. How can I tell my mother this? I know where there's good there's evil, but I've never come face to face with it. I don't think I want to, Luc. I thought Collin was being overdramatic all this time. He wasn't and I feel like shit for even thinking he would make up his moods and some of the things he said."

"I feel the same way. I should have paid closer attention to him, D. Listen. Don't fault yourself. I was here every day. You weren't, and I'm not saying that to make you feel bad about getting away from Lake Lanier when you could. I should have gone too. I need to tell you something too."

"What's up?"

"That red eyed monster mentioned in Collin's note. Stevie and I saw it."

"When? Where?"

"Last night. It was walking with Gemma."

"What?"

"Yes, Stevie was bringing me home from our date when we noticed her. We thought you were with her until those eyes. Those eyes, I'll never forget them. She came up to the car like nothing, asking if we knew where you were. Then, she was gone. The whole thing was beyond weird, Dorian. The bad thing about it is that I haven't heard from Stevie since he dropped me off. Dorian, I'm afraid. I don't want anything to happen to him. I called him this morning and he didn't answer. He didn't show up today and hasn't returned any of my calls. I even called his job, and no one has seen or talked to him. This isn't like Stevie. And, if you ask me, it isn't a convenience either."

"What time was this?"

"Around 10 o'clock."

"Damn!"

"What?"

"Luc, that's about the same time I saw Collin."

"Damn, is right, D. And that's not all."

"What else?"

"That wasn't Stevie at the beach with us either. It wasn't him you took to your mother's house for dinner. According to Stevie, he was at work. I should have known because we spoke hours prior to our beach hangout."

"Get the fuck outta here!"

"I know right!"

"Sorry for swearing Lucy, but that is some sick shit."

"Tell me about it."

Dorian shifted his weight from one foot to the other. He couldn't believe what Lucy had told him. Collin wasn't as insane as most people thought. A red eyed demon was among them, and his wife could possibly know why. He had to find out the truth and keep it from attacking anyone else he loved, especially his children.

"What are we going to do, D? This is serious. We have to find Stevie too."

"We will. Come on. Let's get back before Mama comes looking for us. We can discuss our options later when everyone leaves. Until then, stay away from Gemma."

"Okay."

Tears formed in Lucy's eyes. Dorian saw them and pulled her to him. He hugged her to comfort her any way he could. Sadness overtook him as he thought about Stevie, his friend since middle school, knowing they could never see him alive again.

~~~

Before they went to look for Stevie, Dorian excused himself to read the note Lucy gave him from Kelly. He unfolded it sluggishly when he was alone in the guest bathroom. He'd gone to the one upstairs thinking he would escape any interruptions. It turned out to be a bad idea to go there because every five minutes someone knocked on the door. Dorian politely dismissed them all. Why hadn't he gone to his mother's bedroom instead? No one would ever think to bother him there.

The note read:

My Dearest Dorian,

I'm sorry I'm not there with you today, but I had to go save a life. Hey, it's who I am. I take pride in that, but also wonder if it's all worth it when I come home to an empty house each night. I'm rambling. Dorian, I want to tell you that the other night was one of the best nights I've ever had. I wanted to lie in your arms forever and kiss you until infinity met eternity. That probably sounds corny, but I don't care. I'm expressing my emotions—something I should have done a long time ago. I didn't want to admit it then and I perhaps shouldn't admit it now, but I'm still in love with you. I've been in love with you for a very long time, Mr. Carter. I know you're married, but I couldn't go another minute without expressing my feelings for you once and for all. Better late than never, I suppose.

Dorian, you have opened my heart to love. Your smile ignites my passion. Your touch sets my soul on fire. The way you kiss me, sends me into a state of euphoric captivity and I want to dwell there forever. If we can't have each other in every way in this lifetime, I pray we are blessed to meet in another. I promise to love you forever. Seeing you again after all these years and letting you go for a second time, is something I cannot describe in words. I wish you the best, Dorian Carter. If you ever need me, I'm always here. I'm enclosing my number in case you still want to keep in touch. I know what you said about never losing me again, but life happens, and things change. People do too. I know that all too well.

Take care of yourself, Dorian. Take care of your family and be happy. You deserve it more than anyone I know. Thank you for turning my world upside down when I was twelve years old. Thank you for giving me a glimpse of what a life with you would feel like with a single kiss. I'll cherish it always. If we never see each other again, know that you are loved. Know that you are valued. Know that you are my heart's desire and I'll treasure our time together with every fiber of my existence. You, Mr. Carter, are one of a kind in so many ways. The world is a better place with you in it. Don't ever change!

Love,
Kelly

Dorian balled the note inside his hand as he fought to hang on to his emotions. He lost, allowing his feelings to consume him. He longed for a woman he could never have. He craved her. He closed his eyes and for however long he stayed that way. A knock on the door snapped him back to reality. *Who the hell had interrupted his thoughts of Kelly!*

Chapter 16

Gemma didn't know what to do. She didn't want
Lucy to give away her secret, but she couldn't do
anything to hurt her either. Shutting Stevie up was
easy. No one would suspect any foul play when
they pulled his vehicle from the bottom of the lake
a week after he'd gone missing. Gemma had
planned it perfectly. The town would assume that
he'd fallen asleep behind the wheel, heading back
to Atlanta where he resided and worked. The only
reason for him even being in Lake Lanier was
visiting his father. Mr. Jones wasn't so well, so he
wouldn't be a problem.

Gemma gathered that something was up when
she saw Dorian and Gemma leave Mama A's

house the morning after Collin's funeral. *What are you two up to?* She knew it was bound to happen—those two going off to look for their childhood friend—, but was ordered not to focus on anything other than the plan. She thought about Stevie again. He didn't deserve to die the way he had, but he knew too much, more than Lucy or Dorian realized.

"Hey, my love, didn't I tell you to stop thinking about him?"

"Yes, but…"

"…but nothing. Don't make me hurt you. He had it coming. Stevie Jones was a man of many things, but keeping his mouth shut wasn't one of them. His meddling got the best of him. It's been a long time coming. I'm surprised he lived this long. Truth be told, I should have ended his pathetic life a while ago for trying to interfere with matters that didn't concern him."

"What do you mean?"

"Let's just say, Collin confided in him about me. Of course Stevie laughed at him, but over the years, he watched out for Collin. He actually saved his life a time or two without realizing it. Stevie Jones was a nuisance. Poor bastard."

The red eyed man smirked. He had no sympathy for Stevie, Collin, or anyone else he'd tormented. It was after all his sole purpose whenever he was set free to roam the earth. And the legend of Lake Lanier was his very own paradise.

"What are we going to do about Dorian and Lucy? They know more than they're letting on. I can't watch them 24/7. I don't want to. What about the children? DJ told Mama A about you."

"But she already knew about me, Love. Collin told her. She didn't listen or take him seriously. That's on her. My children aren't to be warned in any way. Do you understand, Gemma? If I hear of you treating them harshly, you, my sweet, will be sorry."

"Dorian is their father. You aren't!"

Gemma was furious. How dare he threaten her or scold her about what she did or said to her children. She wasn't afraid of him.

"If you believing that helps you sleep better at night, so be it. The night each of them were conceived, you knew it wasn't Dorian. You knew it was I making love to you in only the way I can. Don't be naïve, love. It doesn't look good on you. Besides, you knew the deal the moment you laid eyes on that son-of-a-bitch! Don't pretend now, Gemma. Please, don't make me hurt you again!"

Before Gemma could respond, she was alone.

Looking around the room, she picked up a lamp and threw it. The noise it made alarmed Alice and the children. They came rushing into the room to make sure she was okay. Gemma played it off as best she could, but knew immediately that Mama A wasn't buying her lie. The old mother had a way with her looks giving her thoughts away.

Gemma was ready to go home, back to their normal lives. Dorian hadn't slept in the bed with her in two nights. She missed having his body next to hers to cuddle up to. She sensed her husband pulling away from her, wondering if Kelly Bishop had anything to do with it. She would find out. She'd deceived Dorian before when it came to the woman he loved, but Gemma didn't care. He belonged to her, and she wouldn't give him up without a fight.

"Gemma, are you okay?" Mama A asked, looking around the room. She was upset that Gemma broke the lamp passed down through her family for generations. How dare she destroy other people's property out of anger or whatever foolishness going on?

"Oh, Mama A, I didn't hear you come in. I'm sorry. I was having a moment."

The nervous laugh Gemma let out concerned her mother-in-law further. Something wasn't right with her son's wife.

"Kids, go downstairs and wait for Grammy. I'll be down in a few minutes. I need to speak with your mother in private."

"Yes, Grammy," both children replied without even glancing in their mother's direction. They felt the anger radiating from her body, knowing they would be punished by the end of the day or sooner.

When Alice was sure her grandchildren were out of hearing range, she walked closer to Gemma but stayed back enough to protect herself if need be.

"What's going on between you and my son? And before you say nothing, I ask that you save the lies for someone else. I don't want or need them to know something's off under my roof."

Gemma sighed. She didn't want to get into this with her mother-in-law.

Tell her, she heard a familiar voice whisper. Confused, Gemma shook her head back and forth.

Do as I say!

"Gemma?"

"Yes, Mama A."

"What's wrong? You can trust me."

"I know I can. I really don't feel like talking. I don't feel well."

"Gemma, stop it! Talk to me."

Tell her.

Before Gemma could respond, Mama A shocked her with her words.

"I know he's here," she said, glancing around the room. "I know you're here. Show yourself. I'm not afraid."

Shock covered Gemma's face, as well as fear. She didn't know what to expect but knew whatever it was wouldn't be good.

Red eyes appeared out of thin air with a huge grin on his face. He looked almost angelic, but Alice knew that was furthest from the truth. Collin told her about him many years ago and she hadn't listened or taken him seriously. She wouldn't make that mistake twice. Losing one son was more than she could handle. She wouldn't lose another.

"Nice to finally make your acquaintance, Mama A. It's been a long time coming."

"I'm not your mama!" Alice spat.

"Ah, don't be like that. We're all connected in some way or another. No need to shoot the messenger."

"Get out! You're not welcome here. Go now!"

"My being here has nothing to do with you, and I won't leave until my purpose is complete."

"What purpose is that?" Alice squared her shoulders and stood up straight. She wasn't afraid of the red eyed demon. If anything, it should be afraid of her.

"Ask your son. He's my reason and I won't leave until I get what I was sent here to kill, steal, and destroy. Anyone or thing that gets in my way will suffer the consequences."

"How dare you threaten my family! You will lose."

"I haven't lost yet. Remember your grandfather, your father, your son, the ones before them—I never lose, Mama."

Alice didn't know what to say. *What was this demon trying to tell her? Was her family involved in an evil pact or some kind of generational curse?*

"You're getting warmer. Keep thinking. No rush. I'm not going anywhere anytime soon."

"What are you talking about? Tell me! Stop going around in circles and just say what you have to say. I have no use for cowards!"

The red eyed demon let out a light chuckle. Alice Carter amused him in ways he hadn't expected. He liked her spunk.

"Oh no, Mama A! It's not that easy. Where's the fun in that? Huh? No, it doesn't work like that. I'm sure you already know. As I said before, ask your son."

"What does Dorian have to do with you being here? My son would never ask for or seek help from something like you!"

The roar in Alice's voice soared through the atmosphere. Maysi ran to the bottom of the stairs and asked was she okay.

"Yes, sweetheart, Grammy is fine. Stay downstairs."

"Okay," Maysi yelled, wondering what was going on upstairs that gave her an eerie feeling. DJ walked up to her and said in a murmur, "He's here."

"I know. I can feel him."

"Me too, Maysi. Is Grammy going to be ok around them?" He tilted his head toward the stairs.

"Yes. She'll be more than ok. Grammy is a strong woman, DJ. She's tough and they don't stand a chance against her. Plus, she has us. We won't let anything happen to her."

A smile spread across DJ's handsome face. He knew what his sister had just said about their grandmother was true. "I wonder if we can still bake cookies?"

"Of course," Maysi confirmed. "Grammy doesn't go back on her promises. We have to do as she said and wait. Come on. Let's go watch some TV to past the time. It'll probably be a while. I'm sure they have lots to talk about before Daddy and Aunt Lucy gets back."

"Okay."

~~~

Maysi and DJ sat quietly in the living room watching cartoons until their grandmother emerged from upstairs. The look on her face told them that she was fine, but her body language told a different tale. Something had happened to Alice Carter—something that could affect her entire bloodline.

"Sweetgrands, are you two alright? I hope Grammy didn't keep you waiting too long."

DJ and Maysi looked back and forth at each other and their grandmother. Something wasn't right, but nothing appeared out of sorts. She never called them that name.

"We're fine Grammy. Are you?" DJ asked.

"Of course. Now, who's ready to bake cookies?"

"Maysi," DJ whispered. "That's not Grammy."

"I know DJ but play along," Maysi replied. She knew they had to remain calm to save themselves and their grandmother. The only way was to act normal. He nodded in agreeance.

Upstairs, tucked away in the hall closet lay Alice Carter's limp body. She wasn't dead but she wasn't able to move to protect her grandchildren. She hoped they realized the thing downstairs talking to them wasn't her before something terrible happened. Moving around to free herself, Alice sighed as tears held down the sides of her face. In that moment, there was nothing she could do to save herself or her grandchildren. She prayed Dorian got back sooner than later.

Chapter 17

"Have you heard anything from him, yet?" Kelly asked Lucy.

"Not since the night before Collin's funeral. He was fine when he left my house that night, Kell. Something isn't right. I can feel it. I know Gemma and that thing they saw her with has something to do with Stevie going missing. I know it. If she is responsible for anything bad happening to him, she will pay. I mean that!

"Luc, calm down…"

"Don't tell me to calm down," Lucy spat. Her emotions were all over the place. At that very moment, she realized how much she cared for Stevie. It was deeper than that if she were honest. She loved him. Had loved him for a while now.

"Luc, I'm sure he'll call. Stevie isn't one to blow someone off, especially someone he likes. Have you called or gone by to speak with his father to see if he's heard anything from him?"

"No didn't want to bother him, but I guess it's time. Kelly, I don't want to cause any harm to him either. This is dangerous. I wish you were here."

"Me too. Yes, it's dangerous but he deserves to know his son is missing, Luc. Call me once you have news."

"I will. Talk to you later."

"Okay."

~~~

Lucy and Dorian moved up to Graham Jones's house and waited before getting out of the car. They didn't know what the plan was.

"So, what will we say, Lucy?"

"D, I don't know. The truth! We tell him what we know and what we think. What else is there to do?"

Dorian couldn't argue. He agreed and opened his car door. Lucy followed his lead. Graham was sitting on his porch waiting for them.

"He's finally gotten himself killed, huh?" The old man said in a melancholy tone.

"Excuse us," Lucy responded.

"Come on up. I assume you're here about Stevie. No one comes here but him and he didn't come home last night, so I know why you're here."

Lucy and Dorian glanced at each other. The old man didn't mince words. "Hello, Mr. Jones. Yes, we are here about Stevie. Did you speak to him at all last night," Dorian questioned?

"Dorian Carter, good to see you again, son. My Stevie was proud to call you friend. Both of you, although he had stronger feelings for the pretty lady."

Graham chuckled at his own words, which Dorian and Lucy found weird but harmless.

"I told Stevie not to go sticking his nose in affairs that don't concern him, but I guess this time, it's caught up to him. Tell me what happened?"

"Excuse me, Sir. What do you mean?" Lucy interjected. "Was Stevie in some kind of trouble? We're confused, Sir."

"My boy had a good heart. Always trying to help people. Always getting involved in things he shouldn't. I suppose it's time I tell you why."

Graham moved inside the house, leaving Dorian and Lucy there pondering their next move. Before they could decide, the decision was made for them. "Get your asses inside and don't make me ask again!"

Without a word, they sprinted up the steps and into the Jacob's household. Either feeling good about what awaited them inside.

Graham took a seat, invited Dorian and Lucy to join him. Before he started talking, he offered them something to drink. Both declined. Looking around the house, Lucy saw the family photos and family heirlooms throughout. It warmed her heart knowing Stevie came from a family who valued tradition and carrying on the family treasures from generation to generation.

"Many years ago, Stevie and I were fishing at the lake. We saw a woman who appeared to be in distress. We called out to her several times and nothing. No look in our direction. No acknowledgement of our presence. Nothing. I didn't like the feeling that came over me, so I told Stevie to pack up our things and we left.

"Over the years, we witnessed many bizarre occurrences at the lake. You see, Stevie's mama ran off with a man from out of town when Stevie was five years old. A few years later, she came back begging for forgiveness. I forgave her and welcomed her home with opened arms.

Weeks after, she went for a swim down at the lake and never returned. Her body was never recovered. When we saw the woman, we both thought it was her. Stevie never spoke of her again, but I could tell him needed answers. He spent a lot of time at the lake too. My guess is he was hoping she'd show up and give him those answers. She never did.

"The man she ran out with came to town about a year after she went missing. There was something strange about him, but I didn't give him any thought until one day Stevie came home from school in a frenzy. He said the man approached him and your brother, Dorian, one day after school. I went on a manhunt but came up short.

"The strangest part was the way Stevie described the man. Said he had red eyes or some foolishness. I gave him a stern talking to and a few lashes across his back side, and we never spoke of the incident again. It wasn't until the night of my accident that I believed my son. I was traveling across the old Bay Water bridge when a man

stepped in front of my truck. No need to ask. Yes, he had red eyes. When I woke
up, I was on the beach shore. In the distance was a woman who resembled my Sadie. Sadie was Stevie's mama's name. I know she saved my life that day. The question remains is how?"

Dorian and Lucy didn't move a muscle. They listened in awe as Mr. Jones shared his story, realizing that some of the legends they'd heard about Lake Lanier were true.

"I know you both had heard the stories. About how the lake covers a town of cursed souls. Well, my granddaddy was one of those people buried in the cemetery of the town that was flooded decades ago. Look, I'm not a man who spooks easily, nor do I take to gossip or rumors, but you can both bet your asses that this isn't neither. Lake Lanier is a cursed town. A beautiful, thriving, tourist's dream with pristine beaches and white sand, but it's about a town built on the act of hatred and racism.

"My son helped your brother Collin, Dorian more than I wanted him to. I told him so. But we all know Stevie. A man of compassion. Now, he's gone."

Mr. Jones covered his face with his eyes, fighting back his grief. *Not in front of your guests,* he willed himself. "I believe it's time to go find my boy. If you'd excuse me."

"Yes, Sir," Dorian and Lucy obliged. They stood to their feet and followed Graham as he walked them outside.

"Mr. Jones, Stevie is one of my best friends. We will find him and bring him back to you. I never knew he looked out for my brother. I'm beyond grateful to him for that—doing something I didn't."

"No need for all that, Sir. Stevie knew the risks and chose his path. Now if you'd excuse me, I have things to do."

Without another word, Graham Jones closed his door and wept. He knew his son was lost. No one could help him now.

———

~~~

Dorian and Lucy drove away from Stevie's childhood home without a word spoken. A million thoughts twirled in their heads, but they couldn't form words to match. When they pulled up to Mama A's house, they immediately knew something was off. Maysi and DJ ran outside. They jumped into the car, causing Dorian and Lucy to show great concern.

Maysi explained what happened. Dorian couldn't believe the words flowing from his daughter's lips. Rushing into the house, he found his mother in the hall closet. Lifting her into his arms, he carried her to the car and headed to the local hospital.

Alice Carter was in a coma, and two weeks had passed.

Chapter 18

Flashback...

Alice hadn't forgotten to speak to DJ about his comment in the car on the way to the church the day of Collin's funeral. When the last guest left, she called him into the kitchen. Pulling out the fresh batch of chocolate chip cookies from the oven, she watched her grandson climb onto one of the stools at the kitchen island.

"May I please have one, Grammy? They look so delicious and smell yummy."

The way DJ's little face lit up, touched Alice's heart beyond words. She wanted to kiss his cheeks and hug him tightly but didn't want to overwhelm him, considering he wasn't the most affectionate child.

"Sure, baby but just one. Grammy needs to talk to you about what you said in the car. What did you mean by you couldn't sleep because it isn't safe?"

DJ lowered his eyes, fidgeting with his tiny hands.

"You won't believe me the same way Mommy and Daddy."

"That's not true, baby. Grammy will believe you. Tell me. Maybe I can help. I promise to always protect you and your sister."

DJ stared up at his grandmother, searching her face. He wanted to make sure she was who she was supposed to be. Sometimes, people weren't who they seem. Just like the man who joined them for dinner, he wasn't who he claimed to be. The smell surrounding him gave him away. Maysi and DJ had become quite familiar with the smells. They warned them when trouble was around protecting them somehow.

"Grammy, something's wrong with Mommy. She hasn't been herself since we got to your house. One night, Maysi and I saw her talking to a man with red eyes. We've seen the man at our house, but never with Mommy. He's usually in our room hiding in the closet. Whenever Daddy comes to check the room for monsters, he disappears but he always comes back."

DJ stopped talking for a second and then said, "Now, he's here."

Alice didn't know what to say. Fear ripped through her entire body. She could tell from the way her grandson spoke that he was telling the truth. It also reminded her of something Collin told her when he around the same age as DJ. The red-eyed monster.

"DJ baby, Grammy believes you. When was the last time you saw the red-eyed man?"

"Last night. He was walking through the house when everyone was asleep. I got up to use the bathroom and there he was. He smiled at me."

"Has he ever tried to hurt you and Maysi?"

DJ shook his head. "No, Grammy. He doesn't try to hurt or scare us. He's just always there. It's like he's watching over us or something. I don't like him. He frightens me, Grammy. Can you make him go away? Maysi doesn't like him either. He scares her too."

Alice stirs about, remembering the way her grandson looked the day he shared that information with her. She had to wake up. Her mind told her body to move but it wouldn't cooperate. Her family was in danger. They needed her to protect them. She couldn't fail them the way she'd failed Collin and Ford.

~~~

Drifting off into a dream, Alice recalled her grandfather and father talking one day.

"Those bastards are trying to destroy our town. We cannot just lay down and play dead. Too

243

many people will get hurt or worse, Pop," Adam told his father.

"I know son but what can we do? No one will listen to reason. Now finish packing up your family so we can get the hell out of here before it's too late. We can head toward Atlanta and start over."

"But Pop…"

"…but nothing, Adam! People are afraid of change around these parts. This is all they know. This is all they want to know and probably will ever know, son. The mentality of our people will keep us at the bottom of the food chain, even though we are so much more. I've witnessed it time and time again. I chose to do better for my family, for you son. You are all I have left. And I'll be damned if I sit around and watch you self-destruct trying to save people who don't wish to save themselves. Your family will break this awful generational curse."

"Pop," Adam tried to explain. His father walked away.

The next morning, Alice remembered being pulled from water. Gasping for breath, she held on tight to the arms of her grandfather. All the screams and sobs embedded into her mind, forever. It was a day an innocent town flooded, and another, created. A town of supernatural mystery.

"Pop, what do we do now?" Her father had asked desperately. His wife, Sophia, Alice's mother, barely conscious at his side. "She needs a doctor."

"Clara, I know but we have to keep moving. The water is rising fast and if we don't get out of here, we won't survive," Henry Carter spoke calmly, yet firm.

Alice recalled her mother's hand reaching for her. We lay hurdled together to stay warm throughout the cold night. By morning, Sophia was gone. Everyone in the boat released their cries and fought to survive and stay together. The dark waters clawing at them, beckoning them to end their misery in the raging currents.

Three days passed before dry land was discovered. The Carter family and several others found refuge in the quaint town, deciding to settle and call it home. Lake Lanier had been their safe haven since. Up until the day strange things started happening, taking one family member every few years for now three generations if Collin was included.

Alice Carter opened her eyes. She knew what had to be done. No more of her family would be taken from her.

Chapter 19

Kelly smiled when she looked at her phone. She hadn't expected to hear from him when she gave Dorian her number, but the butterflies in her stomach danced a happy dance.

"Hey, you."

"Hi, Kell. How are you? I didn't catch you at a bad time, did I?"

"No, you didn't. I'm well. How are you?"

She didn't like the sound of his voice. He didn't seem himself. Kelly hoped everything was okay.

Dorian paused. He didn't want to dive right into it with Kelly, but he wanted answers.

"Why didn't you tell me that you and my brother kept in touch all these years, Kelly? Why him and not me? Huh? What did I do to make you treat me like something stuck to the bottom of your shoe?"

"Excuse me?"

Kelly knew this day would come, but how did he find out? Collin hadn't told Dorian about them staying in touch all these years—that, she was sure of. Before she could gather her thoughts, Dorian's voice slapped her back into the heated conversation he'd forced upon her.

"Oh, I think you heard me loud and clear. You owe me an explanation, Kelly. Once I get that, I'll leave you be. You won't ever hear from me again. Besides, I have no room in my life for liars."

Hearing Dorian speak those words saddened Kelly in a way she hadn't anticipated. Losing him again wasn't something she was prepared to do. He was one of her best friends. She needed him in her life. The connection they shared soothed her soul and gave her hope that soulmates existed. In Kelly's eyes, Dorian was hers, but was he serious?

No room for liars when he was sleeping with the enemy. She wasn't letting him get away with addressing her in this manner. Not now, not ever.

"First of all, calm down and lower your voice. You will not speak to me in that tone and if you think otherwise, we can end this call right now. If someone pissed you off, it surely wasn't me. Do you need to hang up and call back with a new attitude because this one isn't cute and it's damn sure not you? Even though it's you, Dorian, I won't tolerate this disrespectful bullshit!"

Dorian exhaled. He knew Kelly was right. He was being an asshole.

"I'm sorry for speaking to you harshly, but I need answers, Kelly. Mom is in the hospital. She's in a coma and the doctors don't know when or if she'll wake up."

"Oh my God, Dorian! I'm so sorry. What happened to her?"

"I came home, after Lucy and I went to speak with Stevie's dad to see if he knew anything about his whereabouts and my children came running outside the house. Mama was in a closet unconscious and hasn't responded to anything or anyone."

"Where's Gemma?"

"She's missing too, Kelly!"

"Dorian, I'm so sorry. How are Maysi and DJ?"

"Kelly, please! I need the distraction. My children are as good as to be expected given the circumstances. They're worried about their grandmother, but surprisingly, haven't asked about their mother. They're with Lucy."

Strange, Kelly thought but kept that to herself.

"Dorian, okay, listen. I don't know what you want me to say. Collin and I were friends. I don't have to clear it by you or anyone else on who I choose to be friends with."

"I know but he was my brother. Doesn't that count for something, Kelly?"

She couldn't believe she was about to explain her relationship with Collin to Dorian.

"Collin came to New York a few years ago and we ran into each other. Like literally, ran into each other. I was walking to meet a few friends for dinner and when I rounded the corner there, he was. All bright eyed and charming as usual. He ended up coming with me to dinner and meeting my friends. They loved him, of course. You know Collin. Always the life of the party. I invited him back to my place that night because something on his face told me that he needed a friend to listen. And that's what I did, Dorian. I listened as he poured his heart out to me.

"We stayed in contact after that. Now, I apologize for not telling you, but I won't apologize for being Collin's friend. I'm not trying to be mean, but he was your brother, Dorian. If he wanted you to know, he would have told you. Why does it bother you at all that we were friends?"

"Because…"

"Because isn't an answer and certainly not one I'll accept, especially coming from you, Dorian. We're better than that. Stop acting like you're ten and express yourself like the grown man that you are, please! You men get on my damn nerves. Wanting to have a healthy conversation, but then, don't want to open up completely. Or think it's an argument. I'm over that, especially with you, Dorian. Now either talk to me like a man or continue to act like a boy."

Well damn, Dorian thought, smiling inwardly. He liked when Kelly got on to him. He'd missed that about her—about their friendship. It was something he needed.

"Kelly, you were supposed to be mine, no one else. Mine. Knowing that my brother got to have a part of you makes me feel robbed somehow."

It was Kelly's turn to exhale. She knew it was time to open up to the man she still loved. It was better to say what was on her heart than to keep it bottled inside. This could be her only chance.

"So…"

She paused.

"I feel like I should be open and honest with you—something I've stopped myself from doing even way back when we were kids. I guess it's my fear of getting hurt, being ignored, or looking foolish somehow. But I'm putting myself out there. Truth is Dorian, Collin listened. He didn't make me feel small when I confided in him about my feelings for you."

"You told him and not me? When? And why him and not me, Kelly?"

"Don't ask questions you're not able to handle the answers to, Dorian. Plus, I don't feel like it's the right time to talk about this. With Mama A in the hospital and Gemma missing,

Dorian, this can be overwhelming you more than it already is."

"Tell me. I can handle it. Contrary to belief, I'm not the boy you remember. I am, despite my previous actions, a grown ass man, Kell."

"Are you sure, Dorian?"

"Positively."

"Okay. After prom."

Dorian took a deep breath but didn't respond. He wanted to hear all that Kelly wanted to share. It was long overdue.

"Collin saw me sitting at the beach that night after you dropped me off and stopped to see if I was okay. I talked. He listened. When he came to New York, I knew it was my turn to listen."

"You could have talked to me. I would have listened."

"Please, Dorian. Let me finish before you say anything else."

"I'm sorry. Continue."

"I didn't know what I wanted after our kiss. I didn't want things to be weird between us, so I panicked. Truth is. I couldn't get enough of you then, Dorian. I can't get enough of you now. I miss you all the time. I think of you constantly. I wonder what life for us would have been and smile because I know it would have been great! I shut you out and I regret it every single day of my life.

"Collin didn't make me feel bad about sharing my thoughts with him. In fact, he advised me to tell you. I didn't listen of course."

Kelly looked down at her hands and noticed them shaking. She willed herself to calm down before she went on.

"Dorian, since we've reconnected, I feel light. The connection we had is the same as it was the way I remember it so long ago. I can exhale, knowing you see me for who I am and aspire to be. I've fallen. Hell, I fell nearly 20 years ago. I guard myself to keep my vulnerability intact. But, when I'm near you, I become me. You ignite my flame, Dorian."

Kelly stopped talking. What she was about to admit out loud was life's cruel joke on them both.

"Sadly, you have built a life with someone else and there's only a small place for me in it. It's not your fault, but it's so unfair. Collin understood and told me to first, make myself proud of the life I built alone unsettling—uncompromising. He inspired me, Dorian. Your brother was my muse and I miss him deeply. He was also the most honest and sincere person I know. I knew."

Tears fell down Kelly's face. She didn't fight them or try to hide her sobs from Dorian. Her heart ached for so many reasons at that moment, and she knew that speaking her truth was cleansing to her soul.

Dorian fought back his own tears. He didn't know what to say to comfort Kelly because he needed some himself. Losing his brother was one thing but losing the woman he loved was something much worse. He couldn't lose her again. *She's not yours to lose,* a voice whispered in his ear, startling Dorian out of his seat. Looking around the room, he shivered at the coldness that suddenly engulfed him.

"Dorian!" He heard Kelly shout through the phone.

"Uh, yes, I'm okay. I thought I heard someone come inside the room."

"Where are you?"

"I'm at the hospital in a secluded waiting room." Dorian released a sigh. "Kelly, thank you for telling me your feelings. I know we have separate lives, but I cannot lose you. Promise me we will stay connected."

"Dorian?"

"No, please! Promise me, Kelly."

Kelly didn't want to give Dorian any false hope, but she also didn't want to lose him again either. "I promise," she murmured.

"Okay, I have to go. Something is going on here. I need to check on my mother."

"Go. Call me when you can. I'll be here waiting."

Dorian smiled but disconnected the call. His heart was full, but there was so much he wanted to say to Kelly. It wasn't a conversation for over the phone. No, he would do it in person. Just as soon as his mother was okay and Gemma was found, Dorian would go to Kelly.

Rounding the corridor, he noticed the nurses enter his mother's hospital room. "Hey," he yelled, picking up his pace. When he peeked inside the door, expecting the worst, his heart dropped. There was his mother sitting up in bed with a beautiful smile on her face as if she were expecting him at any minute.

"Hey, sweetheart!" she called out in the sweetest voice he'd ever heard.

Taking long strides, Dorian went to his mother and sit down next to her on the bed. "Hey, Mama. Are you okay? You had us worried."

"I had myself worried, baby. But I'm a fighter. It's in our blood. Where are my grandbabies?" Alice asked, looking around for them.

"They're fine. Lucy has them. I can call her and ask her to bring them to see you if you like?"

"Yes, please!"

Dorian and Alice talked in whispered voices until, Maysi and DJ ran into the room, filling the air with joyful energy. They were happy their Grammy was alive and well. When Gemma soon followed, everyone was left speechless. *Where had she been,* they all wondered.

Chapter 20

Weeks later, once Alice was home from the hospital and things seemed back to normal for the Carter family, Dorian and Lucy went for a walk to their favorite spot. He'd decided to stay in Lake Lanier a while longer to make sure things were good before asking his mother to move to California with him and his family.

Gemma hadn't shown any signs of strange behavior, which Dorian and Alice was grateful. Maysi and DJ still didn't want to be left alone with her.

A lot had happened in Lake Lanier since Alice was in a coma. Several people went missing. Stevie Jones' body still hadn't been discovered, although his truck was found at the bottom of the lake. More souls roamed about the town in search of loved ones and those deemed responsible for their expiration. Lucy thought she saw Collin a few times, telling Dorian how scary it was for her. She kept the part about Stevie coming to her for help to herself.

He came later one night as she lay in bed, missing him. A slight chill in the air signaled she wasn't alone. Lucy sat up and prepared for Gemma to finally pay her an unfriendly visit for sticking her nose where it didn't belong.

"Lucy, it's me. I need your help." She heard.

"Stevie. Is that you?"

"Yes, it's me, Luc. I need to tell you something before it's too late. Don't be afraid."

"I'm not afraid. Let me help you. Tell me what I need to do."

Lucy eased out of bed and put on her robe. She walked to her kitchen and turned on the stove to make some tea. It would indeed be a long night.

~~~

Stevie told Lucy about what his father shared with her and Dorian, and more. He told her about Collin needing his help over the years and before his death. Stevie warned Lucy about a foe among them that none of them saw coming, but just as he was about to reveal who, he vanished right before her eyes, leaving her more confused than ever. Lucy hadn't heard from or seen Stevie again.

When Mama A was released from the hospital, Lucy went ahead to the house to make sure everything was comfortable for her return. Gemma sat waiting on the porch as she drove up to the house. She looked frightened beyond anything Lucy had seen.

"Gemma, what's wrong? Where have you been?"

As if she didn't recognize who Lucy was, Gemma sat rocking back and forth. Her mind couldn't remember, and she didn't want to. Being tormented by her red eyed lover was one thing, but being face to face with the one responsible for all this terror was way worse.

"You need to keep my son away from Kelly Bishop. She's trouble. Her family has always been trouble for us. That's why we chose you, Gemma. We needed him to let her go. Those two being together could destroy us. Kelly's lineage is pure. She's dangerous to us. Dorian will change and we cannot have that. This is our town. This is our land."

Gemma's view of Kelly changed. Kelly was the innocent soul red eyes warned her about, except she didn't have a name to put it altogether then.

The entity smirked at Gemma, realizing she'd figured it out. "No, Dorian was never to be yours, my sweet. You belong to us. Kelly is special. She

263

doesn't know how much of a threat she is, and we want to keep it that way. Understand?"

Gemma nodded, fearing for her life. "What about my children? Nothing can ever happen to them. I love them."

"Nothing will ever happen to Maysi and DJ. They are a part of us. We will always protect them. But the way they took to Kelly that day at the beach isn't something to overlook. She could influence them in some way if we aren't careful. Keep them away from her at all costs."

Gemma nodded in agreement, but couldn't form words. How could she be so naïve to trust her ex-boyfriend? He wasn't the love of her life after all.

"As if you had a choice. We selected you Gemma long before you met him. Long before you were formed in your mother's womb. It's not personal, it's survival. Now go. Go do the task we set before you. If you fail, you will suffer the consequences."

~~~

When Dorian finally pulled up to the house the day of Mama A's hospital release, he found Lucy waiting for him in the yard as Gemma sat on the porch, looking like a fragile doll.

He'd never seem his wife like that, so it made him soften the wrath he held in his heart toward her.

"Look at her Dorian. She doesn't look well. She doesn't recognize who I am. Something's not right with Gemma. We should take her to the hospital. Maybe the person who locked Mama A in that closet did something to Gemma too. I don't like this, D."

"Luc, calm down. I'll see if I can talk to her. Let's get Mama inside and tucked in bed and the children settled before we do anything concerning Gemma. My main priority are my children and my mother. She's been strange since we got here. I don't want to deal with this right now. Okay!"

"Okay, and stop hollering at me, Dorian. Kelly told me about your attitude. It's not cute!"

"I'm sorry, Luc. This shit is stressful. I'm ready to get the hell away from this town and take my mama with me so I won't have to step foot in it anytime in the near future."

A saddened looked appeared across Lucy's face. Everyone she loved was leaving her behind. My mother decided to expand BEAT to Atlanta and would be moving there permanently in a few months. Stevie was gone. Kelly was gone. And now Dorian was leaving again and taking Mama A with him. It wasn't fair.

As if reading her mind, Dorian responded, "You know you are welcome to come with us, Luc. I'm sure Kelly would love to have you too. You don't have to stay stuck in this place, you know. You should run like hell and never look back. Why don't you go to Atlanta with your mother? Nothing is stopping you, Lucy. With your career choice, you can work anywhere in the world."

Lucy didn't want to admit how right Dorian was, so she remained silent. The headaches were worse, and she couldn't afford to have the one slowly but surely making its' presence known to take full capacity. Staying in bed for days wasn't on her to-do list.

"I'll be fine, D. Thanks but I can take care of myself. Lake Lanier is my home. I won't leave unless I'm forced to."

"Suit yourself," Dorian said, brushing pass her with his mother's overnight bag he'd taken to the hospital while she was there. Alice eased up the steps behind Dorian who held the door open for her. She gave Lucy a thoughtful look. "You know he's right. You're too young and too beautiful to stay in such a small town. Lucy Jacobs, you are forfeiting your full potential in this world. Go, live life. Do it before you're too old like me to enjoy it."

Lucy thought about what Stevie warned her of. Maybe Dorian and Alice were right. Maybe it was time for her to leave Lake Lanier. Nothing good had come to her while calling this place home. But first, she had to talk to Gemma. She knew something and Lucy wouldn't rest until the information was given to her.

Gemma told Lucy everything she knew. Dorian didn't believe it when Lucy told him, but it made sense. It was definitely time to get out of Lake Lanier.

That's what you think, a voice whispered in his ear, causing Dorian to knock over the chair he was seated in. Gemma and Lucy regarded him, but remained silent.

The phone in the living ring. Neither of them wanted to answer it. Before they could, Mama A called out, "Dorian, it's for you."

Kelly waited on Dorian to get to the phone. Her heart raced, anticipating the sound of his voice. It had been weeks since they last spoke. She missed him deeper than before, but couldn't understand why.

What she had to say is urgent. It could change everything. When the sound of static penetrated her ear, Kelly began to panic. Something wasn't right. Dorian was in trouble. She could feel it in my soul.

Booking a flight to Atlanta was the only way to save the man she loved and her best friend. Kelly hoped she wasn't too late.

<u>Epilogue</u>

"Good Morning, you!"

"Good Morning to you!"

"How did you sleep?"

"I slept great. You?"

"Absolutely perfect!"

"We pulled it off."

"Yes, we did. Did you doubt we would?"

"A few times, I did. But what can I say? With you by my side, there's nothing we can't do."

"Aw, baby. Stop! You're making me blush."

"Well, my work here is done."

"Breakfast?"

"Of course."

"Be right back."

"I'll be here."

Dorian walked into the master bathroom of his new home, feeling like a new man. Life was good. Hell, life was better than good. The past year had been pure hell to say the least, but he and his family survived it together. After his mother declined his offer to move with him, Dorian cleared a plot of land overlooking his favorite beach and built his dream home in Lake Lanier despite all the supernatural occurrences. He loved this place, and nothing would keep him from it again. Maysi and DJ were ecstatic when he told them they would be moving closer to their Grammy. For his children, he'd do anything.

"Hey, are we having breakfast any time soon?"

Dorian smiled at the voice teasing him for spending too much time in the bathroom. Shaking his thoughts away, he exhaled, feeling like his life was just the way it was supposed to be.

His heart was full. Being with the woman he loved was a dream come true. Nothing would ever make him leave her. They were made for each other.

"Give me a minute, greedy. I need to wash my face and brush my teeth, you know, make myself presentable. Or would you prefer me cooking with a stink mouth and crust in my eyes?"

"But I'm famished," she purred.

Dorian thought for a sec as a mischievous smirk appeared across his face. She wanted something more than food for breakfast. Splashing cold water on his face after spitting out the mouthwash he used each morning, Dorian looked at his reflection in the mirror. Red eyes stared back at him.

Giving himself a wink, Dorian bounced out of the bathroom and joined his wife in their bed. He planned to keep her there until both of them were satisfied until their wildest imagination.

THE END

KeKe Chanel

"Greed is a bottomless pit
which exhausts the person in an
endless effort to satisfy the need
without ever reaching
satisfaction."

-unknown

DORIAN

About the Author:

KeKe Chanel is an award-winning suspense fiction writer from the small town of Greensburg, Louisiana.

When KeKe isn't writing books, she fills her time blogging, reading, and hosting her online podcast Kickin' it with KeKe that airs every Monday night via Instagram Live on her platform @thekekechanel.

Since publishing her debut novel in 2012, KeKe has penned over 18 titles, self-publishing 17 of them. She is currently working on new projects.

Some of her novels include: Silence, Deliver Me From Darkness, and What The L? Finding Balance: Creating and Maintaining A New Mindset. All available on Amazon and other major book retailers.

KeKe loves to spend quality time with her loved ones, watching Netflix, and coaching new and aspiring authors and writers.

KeKe resides in Louisiana with her family.

To find out more about KeKe Chanel please visit her official website: www.thekekchanel.com.